KASAB

AFTER 26/11
A CRIME THRILLER

SIVAKUMAR THIAGARAJAN

eka
PUBLISHING

First Published in India by Eka Publishers 2019
© 2019 Sivakumar Thiagarajan and Eka Publishers
Printed and bound in India by Eka Publishers.

ISBN: 978-81-94-169581
FICTION
Author: Sivakumar Thiagarajan
Editied by: Smriti
Cover & Illustration: Aniruddh Vaidya

The right of Sivakumar Thiagarajan to be identified as the author of this work has been asserted by him.

1st Reprint Dec 2020

EKA PUBLISHERS
#118 Ushodaya Enclave, PO Miyapur
Hyderabad 500049. INDIA
ekapresshyderabad@gmail.com
+91 8008101590
www.ekapress.org

<u>ABOUT THE STORY</u>

The story is purely author's imagination. Inspired by the thought, what Pakistan would have done if they could have had Kasab dead or alive. If a country keeps on postpone the execution of a terrorist, then, this story might turn into a reality.

I spent one night sitting and thinking, that if I were one of the brains in the Pakistan's think tank, what would have I planned to get Kasab dead or alive before he spills too much. At that moment this story blue print was born. Throughout the night I stayed awake plotting the release of Kasab and bring him back to Pakistan or to kill him.

Sivakumar Thiagarajan
Chennai
November 04, 2019

This Book is dedicated to the Indian
Brave Hearts of the Kargil War

Amar
Javan

"We are forever indebted to You"

PROLOGUE

BOOM! The power of the explosion close by took both Arjun and Sunil by surprise. Both instinctively realized how close death had been. Arjun's trained mind went into high gear and he turned to Sunil to signal immediate retreat to safer grounds. Another bomb exploded which ripped their regimental colleague Surjith's body. It was bizarre to see the disintegrated parts of his body flung all around by the impact of the explosion. As if dictated by destiny, the top portion of the ring that was worn by Surjith landed on Sunil left hand and it opened to reveal a very pretty girl's face, that of his sister. On his right hand landed a bracelet from the hand of Surjith. In it was inscribed, "Love you Sur! Come back fast forever -Karishma".

It was in the high mountains of Kashmir during Pakistan's invasion of India's Kargil.

Tears welled in the deeply emotional Sunil's eyes as he recollected the scene just before their departure to heights of Kargil. Surjith high on spirits, had stumbled over to Sunil who was enjoying a smoke and said, "Brother, your face is beautiful. You know why? Because you share, the same beautiful face of your sister." Sunil's sister Karishma was married to Surjith. Sunil and Surjith were very close right from college to the entry into the Army. Both loved each other's company and had great regards for each other's strength. Their families were close as well. But little did Sunil realize that in his inebriated state, Surjith was trying to convey the desire of getting back to his love.

Realizing the danger in any further delay, Arjun started to move towards Sunil so that both could plan their retreat in a tactical manner. Arjun hadn't taken a few steps towards Suni, when the ghostly silence was disrupted by another explosion of a greater impact.

Arjun saw the shrapnel as a result of the explosion, bounce of Sunil's head. The next moment he was Sunil's body crumble slowly and go still. However, it was obvious from the movement of Sunil's eyes that he was alive.

Arjun had two options. He could either slither away to safety or try and reach Sunil and then take the chance of saving both their life, if possible.

Without hesitation, Arjun, whose love for his colleagues was beyond himself, swiftly moved to Sunil. He picked him up and ran with all his strength to a nearby bush that could provide them some cover.

As Arjun ran, bullets seemed to be tearing at them from all directions and he ran in a zig zag manner which was ingrained in him by rigorous training he had earlier been subjected to while he was taken on board in special agents' program. He realized that it was only ten feet more to the bushes and felt that, they could gain a small reprieve to plan for further actions when a bullet tore through the ligament of his left leg.

Seething pain shot through his entire left leg. Starting from the knees his legs were going were going numb and he buckled headlong into a shallow pit in the way.

The spray of bullets that followed went over the pit and Arjun was thankful that his leg had buckled. He strained his eyes to look for a way out when he saw a canal leading from the pit to a dense shrub 200 yards away. Keeping low, he dragged Sunil and himself to the shrub with great pain.

As he had reached the shrub and had pulled Sunil over, a grenade dropped into the pit they had left behind, and it went up in flames. By now the pain in his leg was so intense that he felt they might not make it when he heard the thunderous roar of the helicopter descending. He was about to give up when he saw the Indian Flag on the helicopter. The helicopter seemed to be spraying bullets at the enemies a little ahead and finally seemed to be landing.

By now the pain in his leg was so unbearable, that he became afraid of passing out too. He realized that to ensure they were seen, he had to somehow come out of the shrub. But his whole body seemed to be paralysed with pain. Like the voice from heaven his Guru's instruction resonated in his brains.

"Breath deeply; Concentrate on breathing and nothing else to a level, nothing else matters. Your will find the pain taking back stage.

As the pain retreats while performing the breathing exercise focus all your attention on those muscles that you need to perform what you have to do. Keep your concentration on them till you are in control and nothing else matters. Your final move to achieve your objective should be directed at executing the sequence of events under your control in one single swift moment so that the pain which will sear through you dose not have chance to impair your action. Do what's required in one go since otherwise the pain will with revenge take over your brain and functions of the body and make your actions impotent."

Taking a deep breath, he did what he had been taught. He cut out the pain from his mind and concentrated on getting every muscle brought to the fore control of his mind. The helicopter had landed, and the noise level fell. As he his mind started getting the control of his muscles, the paralyzing pain moved from the fore to the background.

It was now time to make the move of exercising all muscles in concerted sequence before which pain would take over again. In one swift movement, he jumped and shoved with all his might and screamed as loudly as possible. As he started landing, he realized that he still would fall back just inside the shrub and as a final move ripped his star from the uniform and threw it high towards the helicopter and passed out.

Seeing nothing of interest the helicopter team were just about to board. They turned around when they heard Arjun's scream and saw the Corporal Star spinning up from the shrub and it hit one of them.

Hours later, Arjun woke up to find Sunil Singh sitting very thoughtful in his bed. When Sunil saw Arjun waking up, he got up from his bed went to Arjun's bed and hugged him.

The words poured out of him. "Sala Madrasi" I will never forget you for saving my life and will pay you, when I have the first opportunity".

Arjun smiled and said, "I will take a rain cheque from you, SardarJi!"

CHAPTER

1

Protectors of Pakistan (PoP)

Headquarters -Pakistan

In the neighbourhood of Abbotabad where the elite of Pakistan's Military Commanders lived, it was no surprise when the former ISI Chief Ghani, decided to come back to his family bungalow and spend the rest of his retired life.

It was a large plot, but a simple bungalow and he seemed to lead a retired pious life with his family. The Pakistan High Command respected his desire to be left alone, had made all arrangements to ensure he was safe and could lead a normal life. The ISI was entrusted to take care of the family.

However, what was not known but to a very few is that, the bungalow had been constructed a long time ago for the very specific purpose of the ISI Chief's retirement. It had a completely hidden basement with the latest state of art telecommunication facilities.

The basement was connected by an underground tunnel to a mosque in the centre of Abbotabad where the elite of Abottabad went to pray. Apart from the revered former ISI Chief and the mosque caretaker Jaffar Khan, only very few selected knew of this entrance.

Jaffar Khan, was not only the most trusted person of Ghani but also a man of multiple talents. Khan's family had not just served his father but also his great grand father and had grown up more like a brother in his house. Once the tunnel joining the two building had been completed, it was Jaffar's job to ensure all the persons involved in building the tunnel were eliminated and the secret, remained a secret.

What was also unknown is that, though Ghani had retired officially and was out of the picture, it was he who continued to reign in on the ISI through a puppet Chief absolutely sworn to Ghani.

Ghani over his tenure as the ISI Chief, realized that, the elected Prime Ministers were weak due to the diplomacy imposed on them by world politics. So, if at all Pakistan had to take over Kashmir, it had to be an altogether different game plan. It would have to be a plan that would destabilize India to such extent they would be forced to negotiate with Pakistan for peace. Devoid of the UN's backing due to Afghanistan complexity, Pakistan could force India to give away Kashmir.

He had worked hard on the politicians to provide the Americans assistance regarding countering Taliban. The Americans had fallen into his trap of countering Taliban's with their forces. He knew once the UN soldiers were in Afghanistan, they could never afford to go against Pakistan, since, it would compromise the safety of the entire UN forces based in Afghanistan. After all, the only viable route through which supplies, and reinforcement could be made to the UN forces was through Pakistan territory.

In continuity to his plan, he almost got the Prime Minister to invade Kargil. The weak Prime Minister however had rejected the idea.

But Ghani had not come this far to give in. He had immense respect from all three Chief of Staff, and they all had at different times mentioned to him that he should take over governance of Pakistan. He called the Chief of Staff the Army, Navy and Air force and took them through his thought process. He finally concluded that, if this was not done, it's better to give up Kashmir and pursue some path that was economically better off for Pakistan.

His idea worked. Since all three had been regimentally brainwashed that Kashmir was the sovereign of Pakistan, they swore all support to him and the war on Kargil had begun without the approval of the Prime Minister. Everything went as per plan and Pakistan soldiers had occupied Kargil. However, what went wrong was that Ghani didn't expect the resilience with which the Indian Military acted and took back Kargil. Moreover, he had over estimated the pressure on India from world powers, to show restrain.

Unable to accept defeat, a seething Ghani in glove with the ISI Chief, planned and meticulously executed 26/11. The day the Taj burned, Ghani with the ISI Chief and the three Chief of Staff partied and rejoiced. The only set back was that Kasab had been captured alive.

Kasab was the only loose end which could help the investigators trace the attack back to the ISI and this was dangerous. His entire subterfuge movement in Pakistan could be exposed and come to an end. He realized Kasab had to be taken out, "dead or alive".

There was only one person whom Ghani felt, could mastermind an operation of this order successfully. He called in his friend the ex-army chief Qureshi, who had the reputation of a ruthless planner and executor.

Ghani set up PoP with Qureshi heading the Organization, ISI Chief and the three Chief of Staff being its other members. He was waiting for the right opportunity. He realized timing was running out. Headly the other perpetrator of 26/11 had been caught in US intelligence web and had started singing. The implications could be so damaging that this entire siege could expose his complete project.

Deep in thought about what to do, he was pacing up and down in the basement office when he heard the special secure line ring. Could this be it, he said to himself and picked up the phone.

Came the terse voice of the Indian Mole, "Are you aware that your prime minister's daughter is making a trip to south of India."

So, "said Ghani."

Don't you think it's ideal to have the daughter kidnapped in Indian soil and demand release of Kasab for her return to safety, came the Mole's voice? This way, there would be tremendous diplomatic pressure on India which would ensure we achieve our objective.

The mole continued; however, we must ensure adequate pressure on the Indian Polity for which I have thought out a plan and went on to detail it completely.

Ghani felt the plan was brilliant and asked, how much? 10 Million USD to the same Swiss account, came the Mole's reply. The Mole cautioned, be sure that there is no folly while kidnapping her.

"Done "said Ghani", and the line terminated.

CHAPTER

2

New Delhi

As the driver wound his way towards the International School, he said to himself, another 5 minutes and he could be free of his responsibility and could head straight to the hospital where he was expecting his first child.

As the car approached the school, he got a little worried by smoke flames engulfing their destination. Well, today to him was very important and he got over the inhibitions that he was normally subjected too when he found something wrong and he accelerated the Sumo towards the School.

In the back seat, Raj Kiran, a standard one boy sitting in the back seat got excited by the huge flames leaping into the sky and said, wow! This is like the movies I see.

The driver turned into the street of school and slowed down the vehicle considerably when saw the fire raging in the school ahead. Some of the buildings of the school were on fire. Parents and children seemed to be running helter skelter.

Just then, something exploded ahead of them throwing up a huge ball of fire. Realizing that his rear was blocked the driver brought the vehicle to stop and got out of it. The little Raj Kiran got out from the back seat, the fear, clear on his face seeing the scene unfolding in front of him.

There was gunfire and explosions all around. Blood gushing out from the severely injured was staining the recently laid white pavement and colouring with its ominous deep red. The whole area was engulfed in smoke.

From the smoke appeared six uniformed jawans with AK 47's. They took positions around the driver and the boy and they seemed to be shielding the driver and the boy.

One of them ushered to the driver, "Move quickly. Get into the back seat of the limousine immediately. We will also get into the car and drive the vehicle to safety." He further said, "Please hurry, the whole place might blow up any minute".

The driver was hesitant; Raj Kiran was the grandson of the Prime Minister of India. His mobile buzzed and the driver could see it was from his mother. He realized that today he was wanted by his family the most.

Terribly unsure and not being able to see the usually black cats who were assigned to take care of the security of the Prime Minister's grandson, the driver inquired of the one who spoke, "Where are the regular pilots?

The jawan replied, "All of them are wounded in the gunfire. We are a fall back command in such emergencies assigned to take Raj Kiran to safety. Very recently, the intelligence had unearthed a plan to kidnap the grandson of the prime minister. Hence, we have been deployed to step in and take care of Raj Kiran at such crucial times.

Another bomb exploded close by and fearing more, the driver seeing a gateway to his family took Raj Kiran's hand and got into the vehicle with the boy in his tow. All the Jawans got into limousine and the vehicle quickly made its way out of the area at high speed.

At Karol Baug, the Jawan driving the limosuine turned into a side lane and stopped in a parking area which was desolated. One of the

Jawan's took out from his pocket a handkerchief which was sealed in a plastic bag. In a swift movement, he opened the bag and plastered it into the driver's face with it while another Jawan held him to the seat. The driver passed out. As the boy's mouth opened, a hand gagged his mouth and stopped him from screaming out aloud.

One of the Jawan's seated in the back pushed out the driver, dragged his body to the shadows and quickly got into the vehicle after leaving the unconscious body behind. The limousine geared up moved made its way out at high speed.

CHAPTER

3

Delhi - Indian Home Minister's residence

Rani was ready to go to the medical college.

Rani was a girl of slim poise with a face and supportive body so attractive that she left no face unturned where ever she went. Her caring nature stood out in all her interaction. This won her many friends whether be it in the club she visited, or in the school she used to go to.

However, these friendships never lasted. The moment they came to know that she was the daughter of the Home Minister's Mistress, even the people closest to her drifted away. It was as if she was cursed and had no choice but to live with it.

On the other hand, she simply adored her parents who were lavish in their love for her. There was not a moment when they were not there for her but for the times when her father couldn't simply make it. If she ever wanted anything, all she had to do was point and it would be got for her. Moreover, the love she got from her mother was so intense that she could never even see her mother cry.

She was always left with the feeling that she had the most caring parents anyone could ever have and could never even think of hurting their feelings.
So intense were her feelings that sometimes, she wondered, why God had punished her by placing her in such a predicament.

In due course of time her father and mother were her only friends and she really cared for nothing more.

Her father who frequented rifle shooting club always took her there on Sundays and given the influence he enjoyed; she could also practice. She became a pretty good marksman and started dreaming of a career in the Indian Army till that wonderful afternoon when her mother announced to her, that, she will soon have a brother to play around with.

The anguish that always haunted her was submerged by this new development. Her hurt feelings had a new world to look forward to. She stopped even going to the shooting club. To her it was a very divine intervention. "So, what if she didn't have any friends. Her brother will be her friend whom she will never stop playing with".

Rani became a different child. Every moment she used to dream and be ecstatic about the arrival of her lovely brother. During the period, every night she used to put her ear to her mother's stomach and enact a conversation, till she was totally drained and slipped into a dreamy sleep.

Monica was for the first time was happy in years, seeing the void in her daughter's life being charged with such happiness. Both mother and daughter were floating in a new-found euphoria till the day, disaster struck.

Ten days prior to delivery Monica went for her usual check up. The doctors ordered for the usual tests to be taken and due a spurt in her sugar level, panicked. Monica had earlier shown traces of diabetes, but it was in control. However, this sudden spike in sugar levels unnerved the junior doctors who felt that the best thing to do was to induce pain and get the baby out before the situation went out of control.

In absence of the chief doctor and not willing to take any chances, they admitted Monica and induced the pain drips. Monica all along kept telling them that her lower abdomen had not come down and it was too premature for the actions being taken.

The Home Minister who was away on an official visit to a remote village close by rushed back and went straight to the hospital to find Monica, lying in utter pain. The doctors in the ICU, assured him that nothing was wrong and it's the usual for a lady to have this kind of pain when pain was induced.

Against his wishes, he took the plane to Chennai for an important political meeting, mainly on Monica's insistence.

At 11.00 p.m. the mobile rang, and the Home Minister took it at the second ring to hear," Dear I can't bear this pain any longer and the phone went dead".

Aghast, the Home Minister decided to drop his next day's appointment in Chennai. He dressed up quickly to catch the first night flight back to Delhi.

About 6.00 a.m. the next day, a senior doctor who had just delivered a baby was making her way out through the ICU. As she was about to exit, the agonised wail of woman pierced her ears and she could instinctively make out some thing was seriously wrong.

She turned around quickly and approached the woman whose whole body seemed to twitch in pain. Seeing the sheer agony on Monica's face, she called for the head nurse to give her the history of the patient.

The head nurse came and updated her about the sudden spike in sugar levels of the patient and how a decision was taken to admit her and induce labour pains. The doctor asked, how long? The head nurse replied two nights and one day.

The doctor gasped, "what, two nights and one day", and screamed, "you fool get the emergency crew ready for a caesarean. The doctor, whose adrenaline was pumping, realized the emergency on hand and took a deep breath to control herself and commanded the head nurse to get the permission from the husband for an immediate caesarean. Doing that she she ordered for an ECG to be done immediately.

The Home Minister had just landed in Delhi when the call from the hospital came asking him to immediately come to the hospital. The tired Home Minister immediately redirected his driver to the hospital and wondered if it was his sins that were catching up to destroy the small world, he had created within himself to capture some joy in life.

By now Monica turbulent and no longer able to hold the pain was wailing loudly. In somewhat an inebriated state because of pain killers, she could see the ECG machine being rolled in and a new doctor giving stern instructions all around. Rani's anticipatory happy face came weaving in now and then and she said to herself "it's ok". All this will be over soon and tried to compose herself.

The ECG straps were on to her and she felt confident that the new doctor who looked to know her job will take care of the situation. An experienced ECG technician went about his job professionally and the doctor whose eyes never left the ECG monitor suddenly shouted, "move the patient into the Operation Theatre" and decided to take the risk of a caesarean without the signature of the father. Having given the order, she was just about to move into the OT area to change her dress, when the Home Minister barged in, anxiously enquiring what happened?

The Doctor explained to him that the baby's heartbeat had suddenly reached an abnormal stage and therefore it was essential for them to perform a caesarean operation immediately, for which his signature was essential. The Home Minister was just about to scribble his signature when the wail from Monica shook the entire ICU.

In front of all of them, the entire body of Monica went into a spasm and blood started staining the white sheets. The baby was gone.

Events after that were bizarre. Only thing that the fatigued home minister could do was to gather Rani into him arms and incoherently make his way to their home.

Time went by. The Home Minister and Monica tried to reconcile with the situation and went about their usual work trying to take away Rani's pain.

What they didn't know was that, Rani had overheard nurses talking that the doctors have goofed it up. When she heard it, she couldn't initially believe it.

She lost herself in the internet trying to understand what all could happen in the delivery of a baby and by the time she satisfied herself, she decided that destiny had curved an objective for herself.

She decided that she will become a Gynaecologist and Obstetrics and never let any baby (her friend) go away due to wrong diligence. Though she had shown no signs of interest in Science, her parents were surprised to see her choose science in the stream determination class of +10.

They were equally surprised by her marks which got her into the medical college simply on merit alone.

And today was the beginning of the final examination that will take her to that objective of her pursuit to take care of ensuring that never did any other woman had to bear what her mother had to bear.

Rani and her mother were waiting for the car to return after dropping the Home Minister for an unexpected appointment. The car had to take Rani to the college, and it was getting late.

Rani's mother Monica was growing tenser by the moment about the delay. In her assessment, the car should have come back, 15 minutes earlier.

She couldn't stop exclaiming loudly "Where is the dammed car".

The familiarity of their car honking was welcome, and the car made its way into the compound.

Monica and Rani came out the house and Rani got into the car.

Noticing a change in the driver's voice when he wished them "Good Morning", Monica asked "Gopal, what happened to your voice".

Gopal replied, "Madam, I have a bad throat and therefore not able to speak properly". Stating it was getting late for Rani's exam he gestured Rani to get into the car quickly and told Monica that he will come back after dropping her.

Just then Monica's mobile rang, and it was the home minister from the airport. The Home Minister asked Monica to the phone to Rani so that he could wish her best of luck

Rani took the phone and heard her father wishing her all the best for her examination. She said, "Thank you, Daddy" to which the HM said, "I will see you tomorrow", and disconnected the phone.

Bye mummy, said Rani, and the car started moving. Rani's mother noticed something odd about the driver's behaviour but since the car's front was shielded from the back with a shaded film, she was not able to make out anything.

Rani noticed that the driver took a different road and told him "Chacha, you are taking the wrong road", as she sipped her usual energy drink.

As Rani sipped her drink, she became drowsy and went into a deep slumber.

CHAPTER

4

Mumbai - Chief Minister's office

The Chief Minister of Maharashtra – Kestikar, was relaxing in his office at 10.30am during his coffee break. He was a people's man and his only ambition was to serve the people honestly and diligently.

He had never aspired for a political position. He was more than happy to shoulder the heavy responsibility of running a complete branch of a huge multinational company which he revelled in.

It was then that his close friend Shinde, who was the earlier Chief Minister of Maharashtra, invited him to join his endeavour in serving the people. They were not just friends. They respected each other's views which were very strong though they disagreed in many matters. However, their maturity was such order that they never let their opinions go beyond discussions and continued their friendly relationship earnestly.

All was well till one day when his wife had asked him to use his relationship with his friend to get them a plot which was being auctioned. He pointblank told her that he can never do that. It snowballed into a week's fight between them.

The Chief Minister was aware of his friend's predicament through their wives' interaction. He felt that, maybe, his friend was unnecessarily adamant. However, he was unwilling to do anything that might damage their relationship.

Finally, to him it looked like God favoured his decision. The management of his company rewarded his tremendous contribution with such a bonus that easily allowed him to buy a private property close to the one that was being offered at concessional rate.

Even though the rate was far higher than what the auction would fetch close by, he made his decision. He didn't inform his wife about the bonus he got but negotiated hard with the private property close by and bought it at a price far higher than ones prevailing. He was happy that he had bought the plot on his own efforts and did not have to compromise on his integrity.

Having finished the formalities to buy the property, he gathered the documents and went to the temple to thank God for the timely help. From there he made his way home.

His wife neither opened the door nor was to be seen. Neither could he find his son anywhere. His wife had gone to the drop their son in the school as he was scheduled to join his school mates on a wild life camp.

The prasad he got the temple for some reason had satisfied his hunger and he had no further appetite. Despite their indifferences, both he and his wife had always sat together with the son for dinner. They made sure that Vijaykar never felt anything was wrong between them. However, today, for the first time he felt if he did not express his unhappiness with the situation he had been put in, his family might never understand him. He felt lonely and somehow let down. He sat down on the table and penned down a note to his wife.

It read:

"Hi dear, I have got you something more than what you wanted. But please never ever ask me to compromise on integrity of the position I hold, since it will reflect on my family as well on you. The foremost to be affected would be you and then our precious son Vijaykar, God has blessed us with. I have had a hard week pursuing all these and therefore *have no more energy to sit even for dinner. Forgive me because for the first time after the discord between us I have resorted to my earlier habit of having a couple of drinks. I am drunk and do not wish to do anything untoward, especially in front of you and Vijaykar, who mean the world to me".*

Dropping of Vijaykar, his wife came home to find the note written by her husband.

Initially, she couldn't believe that they had a property in that place which she had always dreamt off. However, the substance of the note hit her deeply as she read through it. Slowly, it overwhelmed her that her husband had without compromising on his integrity had made her dreams come through. Though she had no idea what the cost could have been she realized that the difficult predicament she had put her husband in to satisfy herself.

She opened the door to her bedroom and could instinctively feel that her husband was not asleep. She changed into her night suit did something she otherwise could have never done. She placed her head on her husband's feet and cried out loudly, I am sorry my love. I have learnt. I will never ever act the same way again.

Since their union had become so strong that nothing could ever even create the smallest of discord between them. They were an extremely close-knit family and Vijaykar to them was a gift of the God. He was after all, born to them after 15 years of marriage and many a penance by Vijaykar's mother.

CHAPTER

5

Shinde's insistence that Kestikar join him in politics, grew every time they met. One day when he couldn't fend of his friend's insistence, he very reluctantly agreed to quit his job and join the ranks of the party.

He put in his resignation in the company he worked for and after the notice period joined the ranks of the party.

Two things worked in his favour. He was a chosen man of the Chief Minister, apart from his being his close friend and that itself gave him prominence in the party. Secondly his candid views, total commitment and powerful rhetoric, was precisely what was needed and his ascendance to higher echelons was only natural.

Everything changed one day. The Chief Minister suffered a massive heart attack. After a week's stay in the ICU and slight recovery he was brought home. Top party officials kept vigil in front of his room. A day after his shift to his residence, the Chief Minister summoned all the top officials of the party and in unequivocal terms passed on instructions that on event of his sudden demise, if ever the party believed and respected him, his friend Kestikar should be made the Chief Minister. Surprised, but with all the reverence they had to their chief who had taken care of all of them, they unanimously accepted his suggestion and promised their support.

The same day through a formal party meeting the Chief Minister appointed his friend as the deputy chief minister.

The Chief Minister grew very weak. After two days, told his followers from his bed, "my days have come to an end! Now it's for you people to live up to your promise and make Kestikar the next Chief Minister". The same night the Chief Minister breathed his last.

Living up to their promise the party members did what was required to make Kestikar their new Party Chief and the Chief Minister of Maharashtra.

When the top brass of the party called Kestikar to tell him that the Chief Minister had passed away and the party had decided to make him the successor to the Chief Minister's position, Kestikar was dumfounded and choose to cut himself off from his party till he could respond appropriately.

However, within the next couple of hours he got a message that the Chief of the party had summoned him immediately on an emergency, whatever, be his decision.

All his feelings were to resign from the party and move away since his friend who had almost forced him to come into the party ranks was no more. He still had an offer from his earlier company to join them back any day. He decided to quit and move things to get back into his earlier job.

He didn't get a chance to resign. As he entered and took his usual seat in the party headquarters, all stood up and a member proposed for him to be made the Chief Minister. The proposal was seconded and adopted before he could even try and tell them that he would like to resign.

His total belief in God and destiny moved him to ask for a few minutes of privacy and retreated to the small room attached to the conference hall.

He tried resorting to meditation in hope of clearing his mind to take a proper decision. As he closed his eyes, the face of his friend came floating through and asked, do you know why I insisted that you join our party? It's because I saw in you something which could contribute greatly to our society. So, don't let me down and take up the post. Having said this, the face retreated, slowly repeating, "take up the post". It will do good to everyone.

As he rambled with whatever was happening to him, the powerful intellect of his friend who had chosen him to be blessed with the mantle was foremost in mind. And then came the realization that he could also seriously contribute to the progress of his country.

It was literally an awakening. After deep thinking he finally decided to take off from where his friend had left. In the process of taking this decision, he vowed to himself that he will follow the fundamental rule that appealed to him i.e. do what you feel is right and do nothing that is wrong.

He promised to himself that though he has gained entry into high level politics, he would never loose his basic values.

He went back to his seat and nodded his acceptance.

Politics was in turmoil. But Kestikar's strong decisions seemed to work and the party was back on track. The proof of pudding was people's approval and the party loved his presence for that.

The phone reserved for his wife rang and he heard as he picked it up, "Kesh, something's wrong. Vijaykar has not returned from the swimming pool to which he had gone."

By now seasoned to what ever happens, the Chief Minister responded "Don't worry. He should have gone to the hotel to eat his favourite vada pav. He always craves for it after swimming."

However, noticing her tension, he said "Phone me if he does not turn up in one more hour. By the way, did you try reaching him on his mobile?"

The Chief Minister's wife replied, "his mobile is switched off". He always does it when he is in the swimming pool. Maybe as you said, we should wait for some more time instead of unduly worrying."

Vijaykar, a lanky lad was handsome and adorable. The dark fluffy hair on his well-groomed head and the dark black eyes set in the fair complexion of a face was the envy of his friends.

Today, as usual without wasting any time, he had got into the pool and went about his strokes. He had mastered freestyle and was practicing perfecting the breast stroke which he had been trying for quite some time, unsuccessfully. Today his strokes were not in. It dawned on him that nothing would ever be the same.

He had without his parent's knowledge fallen in love with a girl who was not just beautiful but the very presence of him paralyzed his usually composed figure.

She was a real beauty. To him she was a fairy out of the tale and maiden that God had created for him alone. The Girl's name was Soni.

She was his class mate in primary school and later in their preferred graduation course of Business Administration. She had several boy friends and he had gone out of the way to woo her.

Finally, after several attempts, results seemed to be coming his way. A month ago, she had agreed to accompany him for lunch and they even got close enough to feel each other. Vijaykar was simply on top of the world.

However, everything changed the day before. In their usual luncheon session Soni asked him to use his father's influence and get her sister into the medical college. At first, he couldn't believe what she had asked. He was stunned and when she repeated her request he said simply said, forget it. I can never ask my father to do this.

What happened next was unbelievable. Soni simply got up and said, if you can't even do this for me, I wonder how you can meet my expectations and walked away.

The stark reality of her demand made him recoil. Not only was he hurt but also angry for having got himself into this funny position. It was not the rejection but the fool he became because of his infatuation, that hurt him the most.

Moving away, Vijaykar couldn't help feeling sick. His mind reminded him of his responsibility towards his parents and he felt deeply ashamed. To add fuel to the fire, as he had walked into the college this morning, he saw Soni in the company of her earlier boy friend and it hurt him all the more.

He realized it was pointless trying to concentrate on breast stroke today and got out of the pool after 15 minutes. In the change room he stripped of his wet clothes and had just worn his dress when something stung his shoulder and he could feel himself falling to the ground. He could make out faintly that two men were laying him to the ground.

Vikas and Subash who were Vijaykar's friends walked into the change room to find Vijaykar on the floor.

What happened to him? Subash asked of the two men looking down at Vijaykar.

One of them replied," this boy suddenly passed out and fell on the floor. So, we have called for an ambulance and are waiting for it.

Subash asked, "Who are you?"

We belong to the security of the Chief Minister's office, came the reply.

Both Subash and Vikas were relieved that professional help was there to help their friend.

Within minutes, an ambulance came right up to the dressing room and Vijaykar was carried and put into the ambulance.

By the time Subash and Vikas dressed and came out, the ambulance was no where to be seen.

Subash asked of Vikas, "Now what do we do'? He also remarked, is it not strange that the people who said they belonged to security of the Chief Minister's office mention Vijaykar as, "this boy"?

Alarmed, Vikas said, let's go back to the swimming pool office and use their phone to inform Vijaykar's mother about what has happened.

They tried phoning Vijaykar's home, but the phone remained unanswered.

In the meanwhile, the phone at the swimming pool office rang and it was Vijaykar's mother on phone. The chief minister's wife was inquiring with the manager of the pool if Vijaykar had left.

Subash listening to the conversation, took the phone from the manger and told "Aunty, Vijaykar had passed out and was lying unconscious on the floor. Two men claiming they were security personnel from the Chief Minister's office were waiting for an ambulance to take him to the hospital.

The Chief Minister's wife screamed over the phone, "Which hospital has Vijaykar been taken too?" Subash replied, "Since they were from the Chief Minister's security force" we didn't ask any further questions.

The Chief Minister's wife unable to control herself banged down the phone. The Chief Minister was in a meeting with his chief of staff discussing about allotment of a housing board tender. The special phone reserved for his wife rang. The chief minister said, "Just a moment, it is my wife again," and picked up the phone.

The shock in his face was apparent when he heard his wife uncontrollably sobbing and screaming that their son has been taken by some unknown people.

Secretary to the Chief Minister adjourned the meeting.

CHAPTER

6

The shock on the face of Kaushik, the chief assistant of the Prime Minister was apparent. The telephonic call seemed to have caught Kaushik off the guard. Kaushik went and knocked the door to PM's office and entered the room without waiting for permission.

The Prime Minister was in deep thought over some paper in his hand.

The way Kaushik entered without waiting for his permission, the PM knew something was wrong. The usually composed Kaushik was tense and it showed in his face. The Prime Minister knew that whatever it was, it should be so grave, since it seemed to have shaken Kaushik's usual calm demeanour. Even in the times of Kargil War, he had displayed such calm and ability to contribute that had won approval of many.

The Prime Minister asked Kaushik, "Why are you so tense? What happened?"

"Mr. Prime Minister, for the first time I don't know what to tell you. But in absence of any other option, I have to bring to your notice that Raj Kiran has been kidnapped from his school".

The private phone of the Prime Minister rang. His son came on line to inform that Raj Kiran is missing and not traceable.

The Prime Minister said "Don't worry; I will take care of it. Don't do anything. Wait till I get back to you".

The Prime Minister turned to Kaushik who said, "I have just received a phone call from unknown person that they have kidnapped Raj Kiran and asked us not to take any action. They have warned that if we take any action, they will kill Raj Kiran".

Prime Minister asked, "What else did they say?"

Kaushik replied, "they will contact us at 4.00 p.m in the afternoon". Just as Kaushik was finishing his response, the Prime Minister's phone rang.

The Home minister on the other end of the line in a disturbed voice said, "my daughter has been kidnapped and I received a call in my mobile to keep quite and not do anything till I receive another call. The caller also told me that that your grandson and Mumbai's chief minister's son have also been kidnapped and were under their captivity". The Prime Minister and the Home Minister after a brief discussion decided that they should wait for the next call from the kidnappers.

The Chief Minister of Mumbai called Kaushik on his mobile and informed that his son looks to have been kidnapped and that his wife was told that she will be contacted shortly."

On a conference call The Prime Minister, The Home Minister and the Chief Minister decided to wait for the PHONE CALL, before taking any decision.

CHAPTER

7

Monica was very worried about her daughter and terribly distressed. She did not know what to do. The home minister was already on his way to the Prime Minister's Office and will be meeting the Prime Minister in any time now.

Monica's mobile phone rang. She sprang to take the mobile.

A gruff voice one the other end said "Your daughter is safe. If you do exactly as we say, you will receive your daughter back alive. Or else, you will get her severed limbs one after other". At the background she could hear her Rani crying "MOMMMEEEE". Then the gruff voice said, "You will tell your husband to make arrangements to release KASAB or your daughter will suffer very badly before we finish her off".

Monica screamed over the phone "No No, please tell me what to do?"

The gruff voice said "Call your husband and tell him to persuade the Prime Minister to make arrangements to have Kasab released immediately. We know that your husband is on the way to meet the Prime Minister". Monica pleaded, "I will contact my husband immediately and tell him that. Please don't hurt my child."

Mumbai - Chief Minister's Residence.

The maid was sweeping the floor. Her mobile rang. A gruff voice asked for the chief minister's wife.

'Memsab, somebody is asking for you.' The Chief Minister's wife was tense and did not know what to do. The chief minister was on the way to Delhi to meet the Prime Minister on a chartered flight.

She grabbed the phone from the maid and said "Yes"

Vijaykar's voice came on the phone "Mummy don't worry about me, I am fine"

The Chief Minister 's wife cried "VIJAYKAR."

The Chief Minister's wife jumped out of her skin when she heard another gruff voice over the phone, "Ask your husband to make arrangements to release the KASAB. If its not done then be sure that you will never ever see your son again."

The Chief Minister's wife cried "Don't do that, I will do as you have told."

The gruff voice went on "Your husband will be meeting the Prime Minister in an hour's time. Phone him and convey our message."

Delhi-Prime Minister's residence

Raj Kiran's mother the daughter of Prime Minister was pacing up and down in a near panic state. Monoj Kiran's (elder brother of Raj Kiran) mobile rang. He found a strange frightening voice asking him to give the phone to his mother."

Manoj gave the phpne to Raj Kiran's mother and as she said, "I am Raj Kiran's mother." The voice on the other end said, "If you want your son to return, ask your father to release KASAB."

The phone line got disconnected.

CHAPTER

8

New Delhi - Prime Ministers Office

The Prime Minister, The Chief Minister of Mumbai, the Home Minister and Kaushik were anxiously waiting for the phone call shut away from everything else.

Kaushik said, "the problem is that they are calling using different instruments which makes tracking very difficult. Our intelligence team is asking permission to intercept and determine the source through a different method. But we haven't given permission since there are good chances of the callers coming to know of our attempt to track them.

The Prime Minister said sternly "Don't do anything of that sort till a decision is taken".

Kaushik's secretary came running into the room with his mobile in his hand indicating that there was an urgent call for Kaushik.

Kaushik connected switching on the speaker and attached a tracker to the phone. The Gruff voice that came over the line said, "Listen carefully, I will not repeat again. Take out the tracker immediately if not we will disconnect, and you will face the dire consequences."

On PM's indication, Kaushik removed the tracker after which the gruff voice continued, "Good. By now you have been given enough indications that your children are in our custody."

Then the voice which indicated heightened anger said, "placing the tracker was not a good move and you have to pay for it. The voice then directed him to phone his home right away."

Kaushik phone rang. It was his wife on the phone. She hysterically blurted out, "Our son Ram has been shot by someone while he was sitting in the veranda reading a novel. His hand is injured, and blood is oozing out. Please come home immediately."

Kaushik calmed his wife by telling her that, "it would be better to shift Ram to a hospital and be under medical care and that he will act on that right away and excused himself for a little time."

After making sure an ambulance had been dispatched, Kaushik bid farewell and started toward the front door in a hurry.

As he was about to exit the room, one of the phones rang.

The moment the secretary switched on the phone, the gruff voice screamed over the speaker, "I warned you once and this is another warning. This time we shot his arm but the next time you do the same mistake, the consequences can be far worse. Do not attempt to track ever again. I will call you back in 15 minutes."

The line got disconnected and the next 15 minutes was torturous for all of them sitting in the room.

At the end of their nerves by the end of 15 minutes, all of them jumped when the call came through and this time the PM decided to answer the phone himself.

The voice immediately seemed to recognize the PM's voice said "Good you are getting involved directly. Please do as I say. Arrange to have Kasab released immediately."

The Prime Minister said "Impossible. Even if I want to, I can't do it. This you should know by now given the way you have penetrated our intelligence."

Came the reply, "Wait for my instructions on how you can do it," and the line went dead.

CHAPTER

9

With a battalion of black commands in the rear jeep, Arjun brought his jeep to a halt in front of Kalakshetra which Zarina had to visit. Zarina was the daughter of the Prime Minister of Pakistan and she was visiting Kalakshetra. Kalakshetra had been fully secured for this purpose and nothing could go wrong inside. The roads outside seemed deserted and Arjun could see no harm from there. However, something about the building on the T corner bothered Arjun and he could sense danger. He saw a water tank which was on the opposite side of the building. He realized that water tank could be a good place to position himself.

He instructed Rita to accompany Zarina and told Rita that he would move away and be waiting beside the water tank where there was adequate shade. Rita realized that that position was strategic since that place could be seen only by someone inside Kalkshetra and not by anyone else in the T Junction that forked a bit around a huge water tank.

Once Rita and Zarina had entered the Kalakshetra, Arjun waved bye to the commandos and took off in his jeep. After driving some distance, he was out of the sight of the T Junction. Arjun then took a U turn and through some by lanes made his way to reach the other side of the water tank. He had carefully choosen this spot as it gave him clear view of the Kalakshetra entrance but could not been seen by the other side of the water tank. Through his walki talkie, he informed the Commando head of his location and cautioned them to be careful about the old building.

He then waited for Zarina and Rita to finish their work and reappear. This was his first assignment after his induction into a special branch of intelligence headed by Sunil. His thoughts drifted to the past which had brought him into this current situation.

After Kargil, Arjun had decided to take an early retirement to pursue higher levels of ascendency in martial arts and was scheduled to leave for Chennai. The call took him by surprise. It was from Sunil of old Kargil times. "Sala Madrasi! Running off without a Coffee with your friend? And then in a decisive manner, Sunil told Arjun to meet up with him at the Coffee House in Cannaught Place at 3.00 p.m for a cup of coffee and cut the line.

Arjun subsequent to their Kargil incident had learned that Sunil was not a Jawan but a strategist with direct access to the highest echelons of power in India. His colleagues and superiors had been envious of him in building closeness to a person of such high order.

Time had gone by and it was a pretty long time since they had even spoken to each other. So, this call not only surprised but also elated him that he was being invited to have coffee with such a person. Unsure as to whether he should be formal or informal, Arjun decided to be his usual self and reached the Coffee House casually dressed. As instructed, he sought the manager and indentified himself. The manager who till then seemed to consider Arjun as non existent, straightened up and led him to a room which seemed cut away from the main restaurant and gave him a reception of a VIP. Once he had made sure that Arjun was settled comfortably, the Manager excused himself and within minutes walked in Sunil dressed as casually as Arjun.

As Arjun got up to address him, Sunil came directly to him and with a very personal embrace said "Sala Madrasi, it's really nice to see you once again". Somehow the warmth of the embrace of Sunil took away all formality fears that Arjun had fostered and soon both were lost in the Kargil frontiers.

Arjun realized that after their initial meet up in which Sunil had ensured that Arjun was as comfortable as he would be with a friend, Sunil raised his arm and the waiters after serving them with piping coffee, closed the door and left the room. Sunil's mobile light lit up indicating a call and stopped after few moments.

Sunil ignored it and started, "how much ever I hope this would actually be the rain cheque I owe you, I have to admit that it is your fighting acumen that makes me appeal to you to join a secret wing of the PMO's office. This wing is extremely classified and that takes over under cover operations, during times beyond normal control. I am not sure what your plans are after you reach Chennai, but I would be immensely happy if you join me in this special wing.

As Sunil finished making the offer, his mobile lit up again and Sunil excused himself for a few minutes and made his way out of the room.

Arjun hardly noticed Sunil leaving the room. The flash back started. Whenever his dad came home on holidays Arjun was fascinated with his martial art exercises. Never an early riser, Arjun used to get up at 5.00 a.m. whenever his father was home and watch him exercise. His father noting this interest started teaching him the basic exercises. To his surprise, he found Arjun easily performing tough exercises and look up eager for more. He realized that there was a unique capability in this boy which had to be nurtured and felt sad that he was not going to be around. So, in spite of Arjun's mother's objection, he took him to his Guru in Kerala to train him in the oriental martial arts techniques.

It was 15th Sep 1984 and it was time for him to rejoin duty. A night before the day he left, as was the usual practice, Arjun and his father were having their usual loving fight. It was at this time Arjun's father realized that there was tremendous advancement in Arjun's skills in the last ten days of coming from his Guru's training. Even he who was quite adept in martial arts techniques was finding it a little difficult to handle Arjun. Arjun adored his father and was lying on his lap when he was told by his father, I must leave tomorrow to rejoin duty. He also laughingly told him, you better be ready for a good fight when I come next, since you would have undergone a year's training by then and I will spank you if you remain amateurish. Arjun replied, Dad even if I am not amateurish, I will still like to be spanked by you and said, "I love you and I will make you and mom proud of me."

Knowing he would not be able to face his wife for leaving their son in a distant place from her, he directly went to rejoin duty as one of the special body guard assigned to guard the then Prime Minister of India. It was 15th Sep 1984.

Not many knew that on that uneventful day of 31st Oct 1984, it was Arjun's father who was also instrumental in shooting down one of the assassinators of the Indian Prime Minister before being shot down himself.

Arjun's father's Guru gave abode to Arjun's mother in his campus and Arjun's training continued. While Arjun could not fathom the depths of his mother's feeling, he promised himself that he would be as sacrificing as his father for the nation. The Guru was fascinated with Arjun and in a few years, Arjun graduated into an expert martial artist.

Five years ago, when his mother expired of cancer, Arjun took up the job of a Jawan in the Indian Army and was immensely applauded for his daring missions in Kashmir. This caught his superior's eyes and he was inducted into an elite group that was used in exceptional encounters.

As Sunil re-entered, tears were streaming down Arjun's eyes recollecting his mother's last advice to him, "Do proud to your nation, as what your father did."

Sunil who was privy to Arjun's complete background was unsure as to whether he had hurt Arjun unintentionally. He sat before Arjun and asked, "what's wrong, did I do something that hurt you?"

All Arjun could utter was, "Sardar, with your offer, you have not only compensated the rain cheque, but also have given me a chance to live up to the very objective of my creation, by my parents. I guess "Jai Hind" answers your query.

What happened next was beyond Arjun's expectation. Sunil escorted Arjun out of the Coffee House and a government car stopped on their footstep. With Sunil and Arjun comfortably seated the car rolled over to Arjun's fascination, the Prime Minister's house from a rear entrance. Both Arjun and Sunil got down to be received by escort who took them to a very special chamber where the Prime Minister was waiting for them.

Sunil taking Arjun's hand walked up to the Prime Minister and said, Sir, meet our latest recruit to the Secret Service Agency (SSA). As Arjun saluted the Prime Minister, Sunil introduced Arjun to the PM by saying Sir, this is Arjun, the son of the man who shot down the assassinator our earlier Prime Minister.

The Prime Minister himself swore him to absolute service of the secret SSA and both took leave of the Prime Minister and departed to their respective residences.

Time had gone by and all that Arjun knew was that his bank account was credited month after month with a salary with which he was very happy.

He had gone back to his Guru and relentlessly pursued his passionate martial arts and mastered the Nun Cha Ku. It was here that he met Rita. Rita was the Guru's daughter and had been pursuing her higher studies in Japan. She had now returned to assist her father in maintaining the martial arts camp.

Arjun realized that Rita was not only very attractive but also as adept as him in martial arts. She had also learnt a new fighting art of throwing a star like weapon that could silently decimate the opponents in close range encounters. Both struck a deep chord and liked each other intensely.

A couple of months ago, Sunil had told Arjun that ISA was on the look out for more staff and if Arjun knew of any appropriate person to recommend the same to him. Arjun had detailed Rita of a special Organization which was dedicated to protecting the country and whether she would be interested in joining it. Rita who was patriotic readily agreed and over a process was also inducted into the SSA. Today both were on the Job of protecting Zarina.

CHAPTER

10

The front Door of Kalakshetra opened alerting Arjun immediately.

Rita and Zarina had apparently finished their business in Kalakshetra and were making their way out of the front gate. Something was wrong. In the flash of moment, the Commandos seemed to taking up various positions and heavy gun fire opened up on Commandos Jeep. Though a few of them got caught inside the jeep others had already fanned out the building from which the gun fire had erupted.

Arjun revved up his idling jeep which raced towards the spot where Rita was leading Zarina. As his vehicle thrust forward, he could see four men hiding in a shed spring on them. As one man grabbed Rita's shoulder, Zarina executed a perfect roll kick which caught the man in his groin, and he doubled over releasing Rita.

Arjun's racing car hit one man in the centre and ran over his lifeless body. As he brought the vehicle to halt, he somersaulted from the jeep catching the third man's neck between his ankles and snap of the neck break was loud and clear. The fourth man's leg had also been hit by the jeep and he lay on the floor wriggling in the agony of the pain he was experiencing. Arjun could see that he had reached into his pocket and was trying to do something.

Rita's kick left the hand unmovable. Arjun surprised that no further shooting was taking place, directed Rita to take care of the man and that both Rita and Zarina should get into the jeep and take cover. Saying this he moved quickly to check on the commandos and the building.

Rita took out a small bottle from her pocket and made the man wriggling in pain to smell it. Soon he became still. With help of Zarina she moved the man's body to the boot of the vehicle and as she was about to shut the boot, she saw something fall out of the man's pocket. It was a shining crescent and attracted by it, she picked it up and slipped it into her pocket.

Scouting around, Arjun noticed that the commandos had done an excellent job of killing all the five hiding in the building but had also to give up their life in the process. He then updated Sunil on what had taken place through his secure mobile. Sunil instructed Arjun to move all of them to the Safe House giving him the directions to the place and told him to wait there for further instructions. He further made it very clear to Arjun that no one else should know about what had taken place.

Arjun and the occupants of car reached the Safe House. Safe House was a secluded cottage outside the city. They had to cross an old iron bridge to reach the place. A board outside the safe house which was heavily fenced said,

"DO NOT ENTER WITHOUT PERMISSION. NUCLEAR EXPERIMENTS IN PROCESS. "Trespassers will be Prosecuted"

Arjun looked up the tied body in the boot and noticed a mobile phone had fallen out of his pocket. The person seemed to be unconscious.

As Arjun reported to Sunil about their reaching the Safe House Sunil told Arjun, "do what's required to wake him up and make him contact his superiors. Make him tell his superiors that 'Zarina's mission', has been accomplished. Employ all tactics to ensure that he does, what's required of him."

Arjun dragged the person to a cold dark room in the cottage. A bright almost blinding incandescent light fell on to a metal bed in the centre of the room.

The cold eerie silence with the glaring light made the man shiver and tremble.

Arjun effortlessly lifted and laid the man on the metal bed and tied him up. He then threw some cold water on his face. The man woke up drowsily and Arjun applied pressure on some specific nerves in different parts of the body and soon the man was screaming in pain. This was something his Guru had taught him when one day he was overjoyed with Arjun's progress in martial art.

Unable to bear the pain inflicted on him any further, the man agreed to do what Arjun demanded of him.

Arjun had noticed in the mobile that there were four missed calls originating from Pakistan. All of them were the same number.

Arjun then asked Zarina to sit in a chair and tied her to it. He then took a photo of Zarina tied to the Chair from the kidnapper's phone and replied to the miss call by sending the photograph using the MMS mode. Then holding a knife menacingly to the man's eyes, he dialled the number and put the mobile on speaker phone.

A voice came, "Where are you? What happened?"

The man in absolute terror of Arjun said, "All the three brothers are dead, but I have escaped and Zarina is in custody. I have already sent you a MMS of Zarina captured."

The voice across the phone said "Yes. We have seen the picture. Don't talk anything over the phone now. Give us a detailed report at the usual time, if possible. It's too risky to talk now." The phone call was terminated. Arjun updated Sunil and was advised to wait for further instructions.

Arjun opened his laptop which was connected to internet in a very secure manner and saw that he had a mail. The mail shocked him.

45

CHAPTER

11

New Delhi – PMO's Office

The dedicated phone meant for international calls rang on the Prime Minister's table.

The call was from Pakistan's Prime Minister.

It was apparent from her voice that she was very tense and angry. "I am informed that my daughter Zarina has been kidnapped in Chennai. Is it true? If so, can you please inform me on steps taken to free her?"

Caught unawares, the shocked Prime Minister said, "I am very sorry about what has happened. Please note that a very high-level operation has been instituted to secure her release and that he will update her personally on developments".

Putting the phone down the Prime Minister punched on a number which was to be used only in emergency.

After five rings, a voice came over the line.

"Yes, we know the current situation and our advice is that you continue to engage with the kidnappers and buy as much as time as possible. "CODE RED" is being activated. And don't worry about the Zarina's Kidnapping. We have managed to thwart the kidnapping and she is under our captivity. Don't disclose this to anyone outside your trusted office. To the World she is under the captivity of the kidnappers.

The voice belonged to the chief of the highly classified secret organization (SSA). The secret organization had powerful member in each state of India who had the state's confidence and could ensure actions that had to be taken in very difficult circumstances.

CHAPTER

12

PoP Headquarters

Qureshi addressed the members, "We have achieved success to a certain extent. All the target people have been kidnapped and talks with the Government of India have begun. It is only time before we achieve our goal."

Ghani said, "Yes I agree. Even Zarina has been kidnapped and everything seems to be going on as per our plans. Soon the people of Pakistan will know about it and its bound to aggravate the situation they way we want it."

Let's get the President to hold a press conference and release the photo of Zarina being tied up in the Chair. He turned to Qureshi and told him to ensure that every newspaper carried the news of Zarina being kidnapped the next morning.

The NEXT DAY

The front page of all leading Pakistan papers carried the photo of Zarina tied to a chair and the head lines screamed "Zarina kidnapped in Indian Soil".

Prime Minister's Office in New Delhi

The Prime Minister, the chief minister and the home minister who were spending most of their time in the same room were jittery because, there had been no further communication from the kidnappers.

The phone reserved for international calls buzzed and it was The Pakistan President. He told the Prime Minister, "please put full pressure on your departments and recover Zarina at the earliest. I am afraid if this doest not get taken care quickly, it might well lead to a war between both our countries."

The Prime Minister replied, "Don't worry Mr. President, we have instituted all necessary action and will soon get Zarina released".

The next phone call to the Prime Minister's office was from the kidnappers. The same gruff voice came booming over the phone, "Mr. Prime Minister, this issue has become International Issue. If you don't release Kasab soon, we will kill Zarina and the other captives. This is bound to lead to an inevitable war between India and Pakistan. The line got disconnected after the gruff voice said, "I will call back."

The Prime Minister sat immobile not knowing what to do? The phone rang after some time. The three of them had not noticed that few hours had passed by.

CHAPTER

13

Arjun had opened his inbox, email address of which was known to very few persons. It shocked him that that his double secure filter, had failed to prevent this mail, which had come from an unknown source. It read ...

"Dear Arjun,
Please do not try to trace the origination of this mail.

I am the well wisher of Pakistan and India. I have a dream. I dream that like in the past, Pakistan and India live like brothers and sisters of yester years and work towards a strong twin nation building both their financial and military wealth that could take on the world if necessary. I dream that this powerful twin nation will stand against the developed nations' policy of divide and rule, which only benefits them.

Now a crucial time has come. Your Prime Minister's grand son, your home minister daughter and the Mumbai chief minister's son have all been kidnapped. In addition, Zarina, the daughter of Pakistan's future president has also been kidnapped.

An unknown organization which is against India and Pakistan are holding these kidnapped people in ransom and are demanding the release of Kasab. The organisation calls themselves as "Protectors of Pakistan" shortly known as PoP.

I caution you again don't try to find out anything about me. I am privy to the knowledge that you are working for a highly classified secret service organization and your boss is Sunil. You are a very qualified martial artist and an expert close combat fighter. He continued, "I hope what I have divulged to you, clear's your doubt that I have deep contacts and know lot more than what even other top-secret agencies don't know. Therefore, don't even ask anyone in your organisation about the kidnapping because they will deny it. They might even have you arrested on some pretext and you will not be able to do anything."

I will keep sending you mails directing you as to how to tackle the situation and help you to get the hostages released from the clutches of PoP. However, it's imperative that you have knowledge of what's building this scenario. There are five cells, consisting of four people each working in India from Pakistan.

One cell is having captive Prime Minister's grand son, one cell has Mumbai's chief minister's son while one cell is the Home Minister's daughter. Another cell which was to have kidnapped Zarina has been killed but for one who is under your control.

The fifth cell is a fall back option should any of these cells fail in their mission. None of the cells know about the others in operation. For your safety, don't disclose this email to anyone including your girlfriend Rita. Wait for my next mail.

Yours, "Well wisher of Pakistan and India."

CHAPTER

14

The Prime Minister, Home Minister and the Chief Minister stared at the ringing phone. The Prime minister pressed the green button and the line got connected switching on the speaker.

The same gruff voice boomed,

"You direct your police department to release Kasab stating that you have a special plan in action, which will be to track Kasab who is bound to contact the other terrorists and for which you have a plan to weed them out completely.

The Prime Minister said that "The Delhi Police chief will never agree to this dangerous plan. He has the authority to stall it for some time."

After a few minutes of silence, the voice said, "Then transfer Kasab to Chennai Prison and make your home minister to influence the chief minister of Tamil Nadu to accept this plan. Let the home minister use his closeness with the Tamil Nadu Chief Minister to agree to the plan.

The Chief Minister of Tamil Nadu is dependent on your help and in hope of help from your end, will do whatever is required. "Once you execute this plan let me know and then I will give your further directions."

The prime minister looked at the Home Minister and the Home Minister gesticulated agreement. The prime minister said over the phone," We will plan it out. Please call back later."

The metallic voice said "We can't wait any longer. If you don't act, we will start executing the hostages one by one.

The Prime Minister responded in panic "We will have a plan of action ready in a couple of hours."

CHAPTER

15

PoP Headquarters - Abbotabad

All were present. There was one more new member which everyone knew was a communication specialist. The Chief of Army remarked, "Something is not right. Our brother, who has Zarina, is not communicating. We have to look into it."

Qureshi said, "Yes, it is worrying me also. He has sent a sms that he is hiding low in some shed and once he is away from danger he will call and update us. He has also mentioned that Zarina is safe. So, let's wait and see."

Ghani said, "Let's wait for some time. If we don't receive any communication from the fourth cell by the evening, we will take a decision."

The Army Chief said, "My instinct tells me that both Zarina and the surviving members of the fourth cell are in Indian hands". Ghani responded, "In that case, our mole would have informed us. So, let's not hurry". The communication expert who had been silent till now suggested, "let us activate the tracker on the member of the fourth cell. Then we will know whether he is alive or not and his location in India."

Qureshi in agreement said "Yes, that is a good idea whether it be risky or not. Activate the tracker and let us know of the results tonight".

CHAPTER

16

The Mole was anticipating Ghani's call. He was sure by now they would be wondering where Zarina was. It was strawberry on vanilla. If he could take Zarina captive and hold her it might fetch him another Million USD.

Picking up the receiver, he said, "Go ahead I am listening". Ghani hated this man and his aggressive way of speaking but his cooperation was needed.

Ghani said, "Its possible something has gone wrong with Zarina's kidnapping. We have got a tracker on the only person left out of the group that was to have kidnapped Zarina, but he is not responding. Can you please use your resources to trace and check what's happening by tracking down the man and Zarina?"

The mole loved this. He told Ghani to transfer another Million USD to his account and mail him the GPS coordinates of their agent with Zarina. A fretting Ghani controlled himself and said, "Done, it will be there in your account by morning, but I expect quick result."

The mole then contacted his Brotherhood friends in Chennai and handed over the responsibility of abducting Zarina and told them to keep this information completely under wraps. Thinking furiously the mole also realized that Sunil had to be kept occupied during this important period and did the needful.

CHAPTER

17

A shocked Arjun wondered what to do. His high secure email id had been breached. Some highly classified information on his back ground known to very few people was being divulged by an unknown person.

He switched on the video to the prisoner's room.

The scene on the screen jolted Arjun. The camera was relaying the scene from the room where the prisoner was held. The prisoner was trying to end his life by repeatedly banging his head on the wall. Naturally he was not successful since the walls had been cushioned to take care of such attempts.

He ran an electronic surveillance from his computer to check and ensure that there was nothing in the prisoner which would pose a security threat to the safe house. He couldn't detect anything.

He started to wonder whether he should inform Sunil about the mail or not, given the circumstances. Unable to decide, he made his way to the communication room in the Safe House.

The room was dimly lit but for the various communication equipments lighting up now and then. Ashley the head of the communication room was deeply immersed with some gadget.

As a routine caution, Arjun asked of Ashley, "is there any chance of a tracker being placed in the Safe Room? Maybe my equipment is not detecting the same?"

Ashley said "Impossible". I check, hour by hour." Unable to stand the pressure of his mind, as a rare instance Arjun directed Ashley to re check in front of him."

Ashley had worked with Arjun many a times before. He had never seen Arjun like this before. He worked on the terminals and found to his surprise, a red and blue light blinking in his terminal.

An alarmed Ashley cried, "Gosh, there is an alien tracking device in this place, and this has been activated just a while ago."

Ashley worked frantically on some more keys and the plan of the Safe house came in the screen. A red light was blinking in the room where the prisoner was kept.

Arjun with two commandos of the safe house entered the prisoner's room.

The expertise of the blood curling scream and kick of the prisoner took Arjun by surprise, but he managed to instinctively divert the force coming at him by the sheer auto defence mechanism, his martial arts teacher in Kerala had made him undergo, rigorously.

However, one of the commandos escorting Arjun, fell prey to the expert kick and he went down like a log.

Realizing the danger posed by such a martial arts expert, Arjun did not hesitate to use his pistol and shot dead the prisoner.

Arjun's phone signalled the receipt of a mail.

Arjun opened the new mail in his inbox. It was an email was from the unknown sender. It read,

"Dear Arjun,

I told you that don't try to trace my email which you tried to do. Anyway, it does not matter. I wouldn't have communicated to you if I had not taken enough steps to insulate myself.

The protectors of Pakistan have forced your prime minister to shift Kasab to Chennai and subsequently release him. Soon Kasab is going to be shifted to Chennai and later released from there.

I will inform you where all hostages are to be held in due course of time so that you can do the needful in rescuing them and then transfer Kasab back to a high security prison.

Keep your mobile phone on at all times and ensure that you read the emails in your mobile phone.

May Krishna and Allah protect us from all evil elements and save Pakistan and India.

Regards,
Well wisher of Pakistan and India"

Arjun looked at the man he had just shot dead. The internal phone bussed, and it was from Ashley the communication and computer expert.

Arjun, the tracker is getting stronger and stronger which means the persons using equipments to track are nearing our abode. Do something about it. It is still coming from the prisoner's room.

Arjun looked at the dead terrorist. He asked the commando to search the dead terrorist and nothing was found.

Arjun said "Take his clothes off."
The surprised commando undressed the terrorist. Arjun flipped him so that the dead terrorist was face down. Then he noticed a scar which suggested a recent surgery and skin drafting.

He took a knife and cut open the skin to find a small but powerful tracker. Without any hesitation he destroyed the tracker immediately.

59

CHAPTER

18

The Prime Minister called Sunil Singh over the phone at 11.00 p.m. and instructed him to come to his office immediately.

He quickly dressed up and started his car.

As usual at this hour of the day the streets were deserted, and he moved his car in a swift speed and headed towards the PM's office.

On reaching the PM's office, he was escorted straight to the inner chamber of the PM's office, where both the Home Minister and Chief Minister of Mumbai were sitting. The PM was in his official dress and he directed Sunil to sit down.

Not wasting any time, the PM came straight to the point. He explained what all had transpired and went on to explain how they had no choice but to shift Kasab to the Chennai Jail in accordance with the instructions received.

Sunil was shell shocked and tried impressing on the PM that shifting Kasab to Chennai was not a good idea, let alone the idea of releasing him to capture other terrorists.

However, the PM said, "keeping in mind wider ramifications of a looming war if something happened to Zarina, the decision had been taken in the best interests of everyone."

Still Sunil seemed unconvinced and tried arguing again, when his mobile rang.

Sunil picked up his mobile and pressed the green button to receive the call. The PM was watching Sunil's face very carefully.

Listening over the phone Sunil's face turned pale and his right arm was gripping the chair very tightly. The PM knew that something had gone wrong badly.

Then Sunil said over the phone, "I am on my way there".

Disconnecting the phone, Sunil told the PM, "Sir, my sister (widow from Kargil war) and her two sons have been shot dead. The people who have done this have also left a warning for me. Taking a deep breath Sunil continued, Sir, I am sorry, but I will have to leave now. I will come back and discuss this issue at 6.00 a.m. tomorrow."

PM said, go ahead Sunil, you leave but take care and let me know if you require any help.

CHAPTER

19

Sunil Singh was furious and in anguish. His natural instincts failed him. He was not able just to digest that his sister and her children, were dead.

He took a special flight to Amristar arranged by the PM's office, and found to his surprise everyone ok but for the communication lines which seemed to have been severed.

He realized that in his feeling for his sister, his professionalism had failed him. He had, as a fool, bitten the bait.

As his flight touched Delhi Airport, the Prime Minister's secretary told him over phone, "The Prime Minister wants to meet you immediately".

Sensing that something was totally wrong Sunil took a decision and called up Arjun and told him to leave everything and come to Delhi. He told him to take the 6.00 a.m. flight to Delhi in which he was already reserved.

Surprised by Sunil's strained tone Arjun replied, "Ok, I to meet you at 10.00 a.m. tomorrow."
He left the Safe house after cautioning Rita to take care and be very careful. He said to her "boss had summoned him he and had to leave immediately." The time was 3.10am.

Arjun had boarded the flight to Delhi and was waiting for it to take off. The flight was delayed by fifteen minutes.

Looking up his black berry, he realized that an email had come in at 3.00 a.m. which he had not read. He further realized that the message had come when he had been talking to Sunil Singh.

He opened the mail and read.

It came from the unknown friend and read, "*Dear Friend, Your safe house location has been identified and will be attacked at 4.00 a.m.*"

The mail signed off as "Well wisher of Pakistan and India".

His watch read 5.05 a.m.

The flight attendant monotone came over the speakers "Please switch off your mobile phones and any other electronic equipment."

Arjun extremely worried, wondered, "What would have happened to Zarina and Rita at the Safe House.

The flight took off to New Delhi.

CHAPTER

20

Rita and Zarina were in the same room at the Safe House in a disturbed state, after Arjun left. After seeing him off, both were wide awake and restless.

It was about 3.55 a.m. when they heard gunfire outside the Safe house. They rushed to the Communication room. They were surprised to see the communication room was full house and Ashley was looking at multiple monitors.

The hidden cameras in the trees a few attackers being blown by the specially planted mines. A couple of others were shot down by security snipers on top of their building.

The attack ended as suddenly as it had started. Rita tried Arjun on the mobile, but his mobile remained unanswered. Ashley handed over to Rita with a sealed cover from Arjun.

Rita tore open the sealed envelope, it read, "IF SAFE HOUSE IS ATTACKED ANYTIME IN MY ABSENCE, EXECUTE BACK UP PLAN as given below". Rita was contemplating on the Back up plan when the second attack started on the Safe House.

Ashley hurriedly signaled Rita to do what Arjun had advised. He said he can only hold the attack for about half and hour and within that time she and Zarina would have to leave through a secret tunnel.

CHAPTER

21

With Zarina in her tow, Rita raced down a half-hidden pathway leading to an old car shed.

Reaching the old car shed Rita, ushered in Zarina quickly and closed the door. They made their way to a hidden room. The room was shielded from outside and no light from it could be seen from outside. She switched on the powerful torchlight she carried in her handbag. Both equipped themselves hand knives from a steel cupboard kept in the corner of the room.

Rita searched for a small handle totally hidden from normal view and pulled it out. A small window of opening slid open in the floor. A spiral stepped ladder could be seen and both descended the ladder which led them to a tunnel. They then hurried through the tunnel and walked about half a kilometer and then the tunnel ended there abruptly. They came face to face with a ladder.

They climbed the ladder and found that it was a house far away from the Safe House.

They went to the first floor and saw what was happening at the Safe House through a binocular kept in a shelf. It was apparent that few people in the safe house were holding off the attackers at bay but it didn't look that they would last much longer when suddenly the whole safe house went into flames.

They came down and saw a wardrobe. There were all kinds of dresses in the wardrobe. Rita picked up two Burkas and gestured

Zarina to quickly slip it over her and said, "There is no time to waste. We will have to leave immediately". As both were slipping on the burka, Zarina asked, "Where to?" Rita replied "I don't know. But we will have to leave this place immediately as this house might also not be safe if our attackers had any inside information".

There was a SUV with full tank of petrol stationed in front of the house. Rita told Zarina to be prepared for a long journey and noted the time which indicated 8.00 a.m. Both got into the car and left for Chennai.

From the car, Rita tried Arjun's cell phone on the way to Chennai.

It started ringing and Arjun's tense voice came over the mobile. "Are you safe, where are you and what's happening?"

Rita said, "Calm down Arjun," and explained what all had happened. Zarina interrupted suddenly and asked Rita to look in the rear-view mirror. Rita saw and told Arjun that a car was following them. Before Arjun could respond, the line disconnected.

* * *

The head of the squad deputed by the mole's brotherhood panicked when he saw the safe house go up in flames and quickly got on to the line with the Mole.

The frantic Mole immediately placed a call to the Well wisher of Pakistan and India and updated him on this disaster. The well wisher advised the mole to compose himself and called in the technical expert in charge of trackers and asked for an update.

The confidence which Benazir, Zarina's mother, had on the well wisher was not known to anyone else. Only a couple of weeks ago in great secrecy, Benazir had approached the well wisher and wanted a tracker placed in an attractive bangle which her daughter was supposed to wear. She had wanted her daughter to wear this bangle on her trip to India so that should any emergency arise they would be able to track her whereabouts. This job had been entrusted to the well wisher and his technical expert in utmost secrecy.

The technical expert quickly went to his instruments and realized that the tracker on the fourth person had got destroyed. Now praying all goes well, he activated the tracker in the bangle and jumped up in sheer joy when tracker he had activated seemed to be doing its job perfectly well. Not only that the tracker seemed to be moving providing its coordinates. With great pride he went to the well wisher and gave him the update.

The well wisher over the secure line inquired of the Mole, "Is your squad head carrying the device I had sent to him with instructions that it should be with him at all times?" On confirmation from the Mole the well wisher told him to tell the squad head to switch on the device and punch in the IP Code. Once he does that, he will keep getting the coordinates of Zarina wherever she is.

The Mole thanked the well wisher and updated the squad head who after punching the codes confirmed receipt of the coordinates and went in pursuit of the same.

CHAPTER

22

An irritated Arjun made his way to the exit in the airport. He was irritated by the way his call to Rita got disconnected and was lost in thoughts as to what was happening over there.

Boomed a voice from nearby, "Sala Madrasi, it is great to see you again." Arjun turned around to find a strained Sunil Singh and hugged Sunil saying "Sardaji, lovely seeing you again."

Sunil Singh also observed that Arjun seemed to be very tense. He decided to not to voice his observation loud and both got out of the Airport and got into Sunil's car.

Soon as they got into the car Arjun said, "let us go and grab something to eat. I am starving." Sunil said "Aare bai, lets talk on the way" to which Arjun signalled silence and showed him a small device which indicated that there was a bug in the car.

Sunil felt like an idiot in not observing the usual rules. He continued "we have so much to talk", but you are right let's first fill our stomach. By the way how was your flight?

Flight was delayed and the food was horrible. That's why I am asking you to stop at the first decent hotel so that I can satisfy my hunger.

Sunil Singh immediately realised that Arjun would not behave this way especially with him and sensed something badly wrong. He parked in a hotel where privacy was assured.

As soon they were seated Arjun took his mobile and phoned a number in Chinglepet. There was no reply and repeated attempts by Arjun remained unsuccessful.

Sunil Singh did not understand what was going on but decided to keep quiet.

They were interrupted from a shrill ringing of Sunil's secured phone.

Sunil realized that it was Kuashik's voice which said Sunil Sahib, you were supposed to come to PM's office at 6.00 a.m., and now it is 10.30 a.m. Prime Minister is anxiously waiting to meet you."

On indication from Sunil both got the car once again and moved towards the PM's office.

Just as Sunil Singh driven half the way, Arjun signalled him that they were being followed.

Sunil realizing the danger since they were going to the PM's office, he gestured towards Arjun to open a box which had weapons in it.

Then Sunil, an expert driver he was, took them by lanes in order to lose the followers. Realizing his intentions, the Maruti van following them also geared up and followed them. A bearded chap leaning out of the van started firing on them.

CHAPTER

23

The Kargil connection of the two took over. Clearly understanding Sunil's intention, Arjun pulled the lever of the smoke bomb in the box and threw it in front the van following them.

Just before the smoke enveloped the entire areas reducing visibility to zero, Sunil took a bylane and made straight for the PM's Office.

All of them were waiting for Sunil. The chief minister of Mumbai was walking around in an agitated manner. The home minister was talking to someone in his mobile. Kaushik was witnessing the stressed actions being enacted by different power chiefs of the country.

The Prime Minister inquired of Sunil "what happened, why are so late". We have managed to buy a little time which is coming to an end and any moment we may receive a phone call from the kidnappers".

The PM's phone rang and silence followed.

The same metallic gruff voice boomed over the phone, "Have you made up your mind or shall we do something which will help you to act early?"

The Prime Minister said "Don't do anything. All the concerned persons are here, and we will get an action plan by soon to execute whatever you are demanding." The line terminated.

The Prime Minister inquired of Sunil, "So Sunil you will realize that we don't have much time. Shall we proceed to follow their demand?"

Sunil Singh said "No way Sir, We can't compromise." The Home Minister screamed, "Sunil you bloody well do what the PM tells you."

Sunil Singh politely told the Home Minister, "Sir, mind your words in these trying times. Please understand that this is my area of my expertise and not your politics." The Home Minister not knowing how to react shouted how you dare talk to me like me this and moved away to a corner.

The Red phone inside the Prime Minister's cabin rang. The Prime Minister excused himself and went into his secured communication centre to attend the call.

The Prime Minister lifted the receiver and the familiar voice came over the phone, "We told you to discuss the issue with Sunil Singh alone without involving anyone else."

The call disconnected.

The Prime Minister came out of the cabin and concluded the meeting by saying, let us adjourn for lunch, and meet up at 7.00 p.m.

The home minister started to say something, but from the look on PM's face, he decided to keep quiet.

When Arjun and Sunil Singh were about to depart from the Prime Minister's office, the security called Sunil and told him that there is a phone call for him. Sunil Singh took the phone and said "Hello"

The Prime Minister was on the line. And said, "Sunil join me for lunch along with your friend Arjun".

Sunil Singh and Arjun went back to the PM's quarters where a buffet was laid and but for the PM no one was around.

All three of them filled up their plate and were ready to eat. The phone on Sunil Singh's hand buzzed and it was from his boss.

Sunil Singh joined PM and Arjun.

Prime Minister said, "Sunil, we have to release Kasab. If not, at least have Kasab transferred to Tamil Nadu so that the terrorist will not harm anyone."

Sunil Singh said, "We will do something". Give me time till tomorrow. Arjun and I will give you plan of action by then."

They had lunch and Arjun and Sunil departed PM's office and went to the Hotel Room and after update on recent developments, went on to formulate a plan of action."

A phone call came from the Prime Minister's office asking them to come to his office immediately.

CHAPTER

24

The Prime Minister was quite upset. He said, "The Home Minister is mad and is pushing me to order the transfer Kasab to Chennai and at least buy some time till you guys are ready with a plan". He continued "Let us form a plan of action".

Sunil responded "Sir, we have already formed a plan. Let me share with your permission."

On the PM's nod he said, "We will transfer Kasab to Chennai. Then on a specified date we will release him ensuring that all things are in place to recapture and take him back into our custody.

The phone rang and the static voice came over the speaker as Kaushik pressed the green button. "Have you decided, or you would like us to start acting on the captives."

The Prime Minister said, "Don't do anything anymore. We are transferring Kasab to Chennai and from Chennai we will ensure his release". He further continued, "Call back in another hour and I will tell you when we would be transferring Kasab."

"Good, said the static voice. I will phone you in another hour's time." The call got disconnected.

Sunil Singh said, "Leave everything to us, Sir. We will do our very best to keep Kasab and rescue the captives without any harm done to them".

The PM after some thought said, "Ok, Transfer Kasab to Chennai in an Air force plane with utmost security." I will give you the necessary permissions to act the way you want and dedicate a separate team with whom you can coordinate to do what's necessary." It will also ensure that you will get necessary cooperation of the police force from all states of India".

The meeting was over, and Sunil Singh and Arjun got into Sunil's car and headed for the hotel.

Arjun's mobile rang. It was Rita. A tense Arjun pressed the green button to take the call.

Rita said "We have reached the border of Chinglepet. On our way we managed to avoid the followers by driving through some fields. Their car being a smaller car got stuck in the fields a little while ago and after some distance our car also got stuck.

We are quite far from the battle field, but we would have to walk another two kilometres to reach Chingleput". Suddenly the voice trailed off and the call disconnected.

Unable to restrain himself, Arjun dialled Rita's number again and again. The third time Rita connected and whispered that three guys had spotted them and was on their trial. She said don't worry, we have managed to hide in bush and asked Arjun to terminate the call".

CHAPTER

25

Rita and Zarina were hiding in a bush.

Three bearded men were looking and searching the bushes about 50 feet away.

Rita then saw a village about 100 feet in the opposite direction down a narrow pathway. Rita said, "Let us go to the village and hide in some house". Both silently ran down the path taking precaution not to attract any attention.

Just as they cleared the pathway and were entering the village, one the three saw them and shouted to others. Immediately, all three of them started running in their direction.

Rita and Zarina approached the first house and saw a stout Muslim lady sitting in the Veranda. Zarina took charge conversing in rapid Arabic with the lady.

Zarina said, "Madam, three people are chasing us. Please save us."

The lady understood the situation immediately and ordered in Arabic, "both of you go inside the house and I will see to it that you are safe"

Both Rita and Zarina went inside the house through a side entrance. Then the landlady blew a whistle and five Alsatian dogs came eager for a game and sat in front of the lady.

As the three men approached the mood of the dogs changed and they barked very aggressively. The three bearded men decided to stay away from this place and walked away from the house.

The lady's husband Rashid walking towards the house came across the three men in the road. Seeing that they were strangers to the place he enquired their whereabouts.

One of them said, "We are tourists from Hyderabad and are trying to locate a friend's wife who was running away. Rashid said since you are new to our village, I am bound to invite all of you to our local grand tea stall".

At the tea stall Rashid introduced himself and entertained them with a special tea. The talked for some time after which the three men walked away.

CHAPTER

26

Rita, Zarina and the house lady were sitting in the dinning room sipping butter milk. Zarina had told them that they had come to meet some relative of hers in the next village.

"While departing these three men started following our car and in order to dodge them, we got into the fields and our car got stuck. These three men started coming towards us and we ran and came to you.", said Zarina.

Since she had got a call that her mother was seriously sick, Zarina had to immediately get back. And then she inquired of the lady if there was any way they could get to Chennai station immediately. The lady said wait till my husband comes and I will make some arrangements to take you both to the station.

They saw Rashid entering the house and come to the dining room. He saw both Rita and Zarina and said inquired, "Who, are these two ladies?"

The lady of the house replied, "Rashid we have to help these ladies. They need to reach Chennai Airport safely and quickly. She added that some three people were chasing them before I saved them".

Rashid asked of Rita, "Tell me where you want to go and I will book your flight from Chennai over the internet."

Rita said, "The first flight from Chennai airport wherever it goes to, preferably New Delhi."

Rita noticed that Rashid was carrying a small hand bag which he didn't want to keep down. But he did so when all of them went to the computer and Rashid booted his computer.

The lady of the house said, "I will get you a cup tea and went into the kitchen."

"Rashid, come over here" said the lady of the house from the kitchen.

Rashid excused himself and went to the kitchen.

In a flash, Rita opened the bag which Rashid was carrying and was stunned. Inside there was a huge amount of money with a photograph of Rita and Zarina".

Zarina was amazed by Rita's reaction, but kept quiet.

Rashid came back and asked Rita

"Where do you want to go?" Mumbai said, "Rita".

"Mumbai! But you just mentioned, New Delhi", said a surprised Rashid.

"We have changed our mind", said Rita, by which Zarina was surprised.

Rashid booked the tickets to Mumbai and excused himself with the handbag.

Rashid immediately left the house stating that he had urgently to attend some important job. The lady came back from the kitchen and told them that her husband had agreed to have them dropped in their car at the Chennai station in their car.

"You are leaving for Mumbai? She asked," seeing the e-tickets

"Yes madam", said Rita.

The lady of the house summoned their driver and all three of them left.

When they reached Tambaram Railway Station, Rita asked the driver to stop for a while. Rita and got down indicating Zarina to follow her. Zarina was very surprised but followed Rita. Then as they moved away from the driver's vicinity, Rita whispered something into Zarina's ears.

Rita with Zarina in tow then crossed the crowded road and bought tickets to Mambalam Station. Rita had earlier noticed that the same people who had chased them were following them in a car behind theirs.

Rita looked back and saw the three getting down and were about to cross the road to enter Tambaram Station. Rita saw a police woman inspector standing in the station to ensure the safety of the general public.

Rita caught hold of Zarina and went to woman inspector and said, "Inspector, those people have been following and harassing us. Please help us. The also look very suspicious." The woman police inspector took her walkie talkie and barked a few commands.

In a jiffy, there appeared ten plain clothed police and the lady inspector turned to Rita and said "You carry on. We will take care of them".

As both Rita and Zarina boarded the train they could see the three men being surrounded by the plain clothed policemen and Rita gave a sigh with relief.

CHAPTER

27

Arjun and Sunil went straight to Coffee House from Prime Minister's office to have coffee in a special room which would allow them privacy.

Arjun said, "We should have a plan of action for shifting Kasab from Delhi to Chennai."

Sunil replied "I already have a plan of action. Let me tell you about it."

We will take Kasab out of the jail at 7.00 a.m. tomorrow morning. The Jail superintended will be informed in advance to cooperate with us.

Soon after we take of with Kasab in our car, a team of four men formed for this purpose would attack us.

Arjun exclaimed! "Attack us".

Yes, attack us between 7.30 and 7.40 a.m. when we will be crossing a specific place. They will fire on us rubber bullets, but it will look very real since they will be using specialized rifles meant for this purpose. They will see to that the bullet does not hit any glass in the care and will only hit the metal outer of the car. This is small trick I am going to employ to make Kasab think that his own people are attacking him so that he will be more amenable towards us and cooperate better.

After all, it is well known that some higher echelons in Pakistan wants Kasab killed so that he doesn't spill the beans on them. We might as well use it.

Arjun's blackberry indicated of a new message arriving.

He opened the mail and realized that it was from that "Well wisher of Pakistan and India".

It simply said, "You are going to be attacked while taking Kasab to Chennai. Take care."

Arjun decided to confide about the mails coming from the well wisher to Sunil and briefed him completely about what all had happened and showed him the latest mail.

A surprised Sunil said "then we have to change the plan. We will take Kasab out at 1.00 a.m. and not 7.00 a.m. as had been planned and told to a special team."

Sunil contacted the Prime Minister over his secure phone and informed him of the change in the plan. The Prime Minister his assent and told Sunil that all things he had wanted would be in place.

As they were sipping their coffee Sunil's secure phone rang and he spoke to the caller for some time and then dialled another number. This time the conversation was on the new plan to take Kasab out at 1.00 a.m.

Sunil said," Forget rubber bullets and come prepared for the worst. Have two cars with commandos lead in the front and two cars in the rear follow us. Our opposition seems to know about our plan to shift Kasab to Chennai".

Disconnecting Sunil then spoke to the Commander of Air force and briefed him about the change of plans.

Arjun was in synch when Sunil explained to him that "we will send the car with two car escorts at 1 a.m. and then we both with Kasab will start at 1.15 a.m. in an alternative route to the Air force station. We will see what happens to the first set of cars which is supposed to carry Kasab.

The time was 9.00 p.m. Arjun and Sunil were discussing the exact mode of operation.

At 10pm they started for the place where Kasab was held.

———————◆———————

CHAPTER

28

At 10.15pm Sunil and Arjun entered the office of Shailander Singh the Superintendent of the Jail.

On hearing out the plan, Shailender Singh suggested a modification. They seem to know all about our plans. So, I am suggesting a last-minute change in the plan. Only three of us will know about it. There is a tunnel running from the Jail which ends up in a safe house which is privy to very few.

The safe house is equipped with a helipad also. You both take Kasab by the tunnel to the safe house from where he can be shifted to the Air Force station.

Both Arjun and Sunil agreed to this plan.

At 12.45 a.m. a prisoner was escorted to the car. At 1.00 a.m. A convey of cars, rolled out of the Prison entrance and headed at full speed.

At 1.15 a.m., the convoy of cars were brutally attacked with bombs.

At 1.30 a.m. the helicopter carrying Arjun, Sunil, Kasab and another four commandos took off from the Safe House towards the military air base. Sunil pointing beneath showed the burning car to Kasab and told him look, this is what happened to the original car that was scheduled to take you out and they were Pakistan agents to shoot you down.

Kasab was taken aback but a little unsure and kept quiet.

The party had an unpleasant surprise waiting for them at the military air base. The entire runaway was thick with fog and the air force commander said to Sunil, "it is risky to for the flight to take off now... Let us wait for some time. I believe the fog will start clearing up in two hours time."

Kasab was locked in fully padded room without a window with central air conditioning. Inside the room Sunil and Arjun picked up a conversation with Kasab.

Arjun: Your own people are trying to kill you

Kasab: Why would they want to kill me?

Arjun: They don't want you to be alive and be a part of the proof the prosecution is relying on to prosecute and name Pakistan as perpetrators of the crime.

Kasab: I am somewhat doubtful of my own people killing me

Arjun: Think about what happened when your mission ended

Kasab: Yes, I know about that. We were promised that we will be rescued after our mission and that there will be escape route for us. It was promised by our superiors. It's possible that they might want to eliminate me now. But if I reach Pakistan, I will be celebrated as a hero.

Arjun: You know that what you say is simply your own belief. Only we are privy to the number of times they have attempted to kill you. You are aware that they said Kasab is not from the soil of Pakistan. You are aware that they didn't even want the bodies of your colleagues who died in the mission

Sunil: Do one thing. Inform your superiors that you have escaped and that you are somewhere in Delhi. They will want to keep track of you by some means or other. I have a suspicion it might be any time now. This way you will learn the truth of their plans.

Kasab: Give me half hour time to think.

After half an hour, Sunil and Arjun went to Kasab's room with a new mobile phone.

Arjun: Well, had enough about it?

Kasab: Ok what you say sounds good. Give me the mobile.

The mobile was given to Kasab and Arjun indicated to him to dial the number pad at the bottom of the device.

Kasab dialled a number from memory.

The Phone call got connected. Kasab spoke rapidly. But after some time, his face expression changed into anger and he terminated the phone call

What Kasab told Arjun and Sunil surprised them both.

Kasab said "They want me either reach an address they would be texting me or if that was not possible to commit suicide at the first opportunity. I have told them that I will contact them soon."

Kasab, shrieking in pain suddenly caught his jaws.

Sunil Singh: What happened?

Kasab pointing to a golden tooth in his mouth said, "I got something like an electric shock from it and for an instance it was hell."

Sunil Singh: Even if you escape, they will finish you off. What you have experienced is the tracker placed in you tooth being activated. As it gets activated the initial electric impulse is what that gave you the pain. You will have the proof in the morning when I get the dentist to remove it. Don't Worry, we will keep you safe.

The Air Commander came in and announced "the fog has cleared up. Let's move now".

All three of them with five commandos boarded the jet fighter.

When they reached Chennai, the dentist who was waiting for him anesthetized him and took out the tooth and broke it. All could see the live tracker.

Kasab was visibly scared. He asked for a mobile from Sunil and dialled a number and said, "I have been released. What should I do now?"

"Let us know where you are so that we can help you to escape", came the reply.

Kasab sneered, "So that you can send somebody to kill me. Don't worry I will find a way to reach Pakistan."

Kasab, came a stern voice over the line, "listen, I am your superior and order you to follow whatever we tell you to do. If not, you know how you will be dealt with. We know that you are calling from Chennai Airport. Go to this address at a place called Pallavaram and stay there. We will have you picked up safely".

Kasab terminated the phone call.

Sunil told commando Taake Singh, "put this tracker into your bag and take a train to Mumbai. Alight somewhere in the middle say Nagpur and take a train to or where ever you feel like. But be always on the move. If required, do not hesitate to take even flights, but be very careful and keep in touch with me through phones. You must keep moving till I tell you to stop and give you directions to any specific destination.

He handed over to the commando, a special credit card with a pin number which he said can be used anywhere.

He further cautioned the commando that this tracker is being constantly monitored and the opposition would try their best to eliminate him.

He advised the commando to keep in touch with him twice a day at least, and detail him about his whereabouts.

Continuing he said, in case you are not able to contact me for any reason, you attach this tracker to any long-distance train. Put it either on the top or bottom of the train where it will attract the least attention.

Take Singh in synch with Sunil's instructions, embarked on his long journey.

CHAPTER

29

Sunil and Arjun were sitting in a very private conference room and planning their next move.

Sunil's mobile rang. The Prime Minister was on the other end.

"Sunil, what's happening? We have to make Kasab speak to his superiors."

Sunil said, "That has been taken care of Sir." We have made Kasab speak to his handlers. Now we are embarking on to a plan to rescue the kidnapped persons."

Prime Minister inquired, "How do you plan to do that."

Sunil said, "Please leave it to us, Sir. We will give you a report within 48 hours."

As Sunil was talking to the PM, Arjun noticed his blackberry receiving an e-mail.
Arjun opened the inbox in his mobile and was taken aback. The mail from the "Well wisher of Pakistan and Hindustan", read:

"Dear Arjun,
This might be my last mail to you. Read carefully and delete it. All the three captives are at the top of a remote mountain in a tribal village at Gangtok.

Captives are with the villagers who have been told to take care of them. There is no way that the captives can escape from the village. The complete path to the mountain is heavily guarded by the terrorists from Pakistan who have established their hideout there. The mountain is not easily approachable since the path to it is through a dense forest and dangerous wild surrounding. The mountain is almost cut off from the world.

In the attachment you will find a map and the directions to the mountain. Some tribes live at the foothills of the mountain. I suggest you make friends with them. The terrorists have threatened the tribes that they will wipe them out if they don't obey them. The tribals have no choice but to follow their orders.

Once you reach Gangtok be prepared for surprises. The whole place is under the surveillance of the terrorists. Try to take the help of your army and air force.

Best wishes,
Well wisher of Pakistan and Hindustan.

Finalizing their plans Sunil updated his boss who was with the PM. The PM wished them all the best and said the necessary resources would be arranged and put in place.

———————◆———————

CHAPTER

30

Sunil told Arjun, "We have to shift Kasab. Once we start on our mission, it will not be a good idea to keep Kasab in Chennai."

Arjun agreed and both went into Kasab's room. Kasab was in a very dejected mood. Kasab said, "I might as well kill myself. I seem to be an enemy in my own country," and started crying like a child".

While Arjun couldn't help feeling sorry for Kasab he could see Sunil had neither any sympathy nor feelings for Kasab and seemed grim on extracting whatever information was possible, from him.

Arjun: Kasab why did you kill all those people in Mumbai with your machine gun?

Kasab: The funny thing is I don't remember killing anyone or walking down with a machine gun killing people. I saw a video of myself in the Mumbai train station. Our orders were to scare the people and escape to the sea where a high-speed boat will take us to a submarine which will transport us to Pakistan.

Arjun: What else do you remember?

Kasab: I don't even know what I was doing. All I knew was, I was caught by police.

Sunil: Ok tell us what all happened just before you left Pakistan.

Kasab: Each morning we were given some strange tablets and put into a semi dark room made to listen to some over powering voice. I only now realize that we all seemed to be coming out of the room hypnotised. Beyond that I don't recollect anything else.

Sunil: How long did it go on?

Kasab: It went on for ten days. On the final day, my handler told me, don't worry Kasab. You will soon be a hero on your return.

Arjun was surprised by Sunil's remarks after this.

Sunil: Don't worry, you seem to be innocent and hypnotised into doing something bad. You seem to have committed a crime unknowingly. However, it remains that you have committed a big crime which doesn't get pardoned in our country. We will see how to help you now that you have cooperated with us.

Kasab: After all what can you do? I will never be able to live normally ever again.

Sunil: That's the difference between democracy and dictatorship your country suffers from. Based on facts you might even get released with minimal punishment if it's proved that you did it unknowingly. If that is the verdict, our authorities will give you a chance to get back into mainstream of human living again.

Sunil gave orders to his commandos to take charge of Kasab.

Once outside Sunil told Arjun, I notice you seem to feel sorry for him. He is a total liar. If he was that blank, he wouldn't have remembered the phone number to his handler in Pakistan. And don't forget he played dead before killing one of our unharmed policemen who put up a mighty fight which helped others capture him alive.

And since they have been given very clear instructions that they should not be captured alive under any circumstance, he is genuinely afraid. His family will not get the money promised to them. The more afraid he is the more it serves our purpose.

Arjun' mobile rang. It was Rita.

He listened and gripped his chair tightly. Sunil knew something was not all right.

CHAPTER

31

Rita detailed Arjun of what all had happened and told him that after getting away in Tambaram, she had taken Zarina to her relative's house in Gopalapuram and stayed there the whole of yesterday. In the morning, she had looked out of the window to find some suspicious moments and a car parked in the vicinity of her relative's house. So, through the unknown back entrance both of them had quickly moved out and taken a rickshaw to Chola Sheraton and were currently having coffee in the Café downstairs.

A perturbed Arjun said, "Something's is not right. You have been picked up once again. First, after you had left the first Safe House. Second, after you had moved away from the second safe house. It is as if they have some tracker on you and in all likelihood, you are under observation right now. It looks like, they need Zarina alive and will wait for an appropriate opportunity where they can overpower you and take away Zarina without anything known to the public for some reason."

Sunil intervened, "If that be the case, it's essential for us to capture those guys and see if we can get a lead to the information leakage taking place at the PM's office. Lead Rita and Zarina to a desolated place at this hour where we can get at them."

Arjun thought for a moment and told Rita, "listen carefully. Hire a self driven car in the hotel and head to marina beach. On reaching Gandhi Salai take right and continue till you cross Adayar Bridge and take the winding road to the left to reach Besant Nagar and head straight towards the beach. Take the right just before the beach road and take the first left. Just before reaching the end on the right you will come across 7 garages the final one having a name "The Book Parlour". Its usually desolated at this hour and my friend Shanker would be inside. Get into the Parlour and tell him to show you the way out of the back side. In all likelyhood, your followers would park the car at the beginning of the garages and contemplate their next move while waiting for you people to come out. Get out of the back side and head to the bushes besides the first Garage. You will have a complete view from there as to what's happening in the front. Wait for us to come and when we turn in keep me posted as to what's happening there.

"Ok", said Rita.

Arjun, Sunil and a couple of plain clothed fully armed rushed to the Tata Sumo parked in the front.

With the occupants seated, the car directed by Arjun moved at great speed to Elliots Beach. As the Sumo started moving Arjun took Rita's call. Rita said, "you are right, we are being followed in an Innova car."

Arjun told Rita, "Good. Keep your cool and do exactly what we had planned. We are already on our way and will meet you soon."

Once they reached Besant Nagar and were just about to turn into the road leading to book parlour, Arjun cautioned the driver to approach the other end in a slow measure.

As the Sumo moved forward about 50 meters into the road, to the right appeared some garages most of which were closed. The sign of Book Parlour stood on top of the last Garage.

Upon Arjun's instruction, the driver stopped the Sumo in front of one house and Arjun got down as if to check the address of the house.

Arjun could see that an Innova stood in the front of the first garage about 100 feet from the Book Parlour.

Arjun's took the call on his mobile. Rita's shrill voice came crystal clear, "We are hiding behind the bushes and can see you. They were inside the Toyota innova and seem to be fully armed. So be careful."

Arjun realized that if the occupants in the Innova were visibly armed, they could create havoc in this domestic neighbour hood and therefore had to be taken by total surprise.

Walking down the street, he shouted to the driver of his vehicle, "don't bother. Those people sitting in the Innova might know this place. Drive up to them and ask them."

The tense driver of the Innova Ajmal, who was the head of the squad, felt nervous as the Sumo rolled past them and then he heard Arjun shout to the driver, "fool, turn around so that we can inquire about the address from the people sitting in the red car."

Ajmal as a precautionary measure told all his people to conceal their weapons and got out of the car casually to meet up with the people from Sumo.

The commando using the opportunity shouted back to Arjun, "don't shout at me" and made a full turn pressing the accelerator deep down and hit the innova right in the middle causing it to roll over with its occupants shut in.

The surprised Squad leader who had escaped because he had already got down, turned to shout at the driver of the Sumo when the charging Arjun hit him on his neck made, making him bend over in excruciating pain.

As the occupants inside the turned over Innova started shooting haphazardly, a bullet punctured the petrol tank and the whole of Innova went up in flames burning up all the occupants inside. One of the bullets from the Innova caught Ajmal squarely in his head and his body dropped dead even before he hit the ground. Rita and Zarina got out of the bushes to join Sunil and Arjun.

Sunil checked Ajmal's body for clues and was surprised to get a device which seemed to be blinking and pointing to Zarina. He took it close to Zarina and realized it was gathering its signal from the bangle which Zarina was wearing. He asked Zarina to remove it and destroyed the bangle.

They reached the Safe House safely without any further incidents.

CHAPTER

32

PoP Headquarters – Abbotabad.

PoP members had re-assembled.

Qureshi informed, "Everything is going as per our plan. Kasab was in Chennai and from there he seems to be moving north". He is travelling at a fast pace. Soon as we determine his destination, we will get the operational team stationed in India to finish him off."

Qureshi looking at Ghani asked, "What about the captives? Can we release them? We have assured our mole that once Kasab is freed, the captives would be freed.

Ghani said loudly, "Oh don't bother, forget them. They are our insurance".

The Army Chief intervened and said, I don't think we should wait. Let's activate the operational team to chase Kasab and finish him off. He dosen't seem to be in our control and this is a major risk to our operations. Other's agreed and Ghani ordered the hesitant Qureshi to give the orders.

Qureshi took his mobile phone from his pocket and dialled a number.

The order for Qureshi was clear, "Your other assignments are cancelled. We have located Kasab who is roaming around on his own. Go to No.756/23, Beck Began Row where our agent will give you a devise which will give Kasab's coordinates at any point of time. Track him down and kill him."

Hussain was in two minds. Kasab and Hussain had trained side by side in Pakistan and they had become very close. Now to track Kasab and kill, he knew would kill his conscience. After all they had enjoyed many occasions together and were like brothers. But then he had no choice but to obey the orders.

He dressed in a pyjama and kurta and slipped on a spectacle. With a red colour beaded necklace around his neck and a bag in his shoulder he went outside and took a cab.

He told the driver in a very polite voice, "Please, take me to Beck Began Row."

When they reached Beck Bagan Row, Hussain got down and walked towards the end of the road.

He reached No.23. It took nothing but a glance at the girls parading in front of the house that it was a whore joint. When they saw Hussain, they bee lined and offered themselves to him in hope of an evening treat. A very authoritative lady suddenly made her appearance and ordered something in Bengali which sent the girls scampering back to their posts.

The madam invited Hussain to come inside and offered him tea.

With Hussain seated and sipping his cup, Madam said, "the eyes of some insect, and waited"

A prepared Hussain completed, "the cricket sees through it's legs". After all, Hussain had been well trained in such codes long before.

The madam smiled and handed over a smart GPS instrument. He pocketed it and left the place without any further conversation.

CHAPTER

33

Hussain entered his room and opened the instrument which was given to him. It displayed a map of India in the screen and a red star was blinking near Nagpur.

Hussain picked up his suitcase which was always kept ready for such sudden departures.

On his way out, he called his assistant Rajak and told him to book the first available flight to Nagpur and inform him.

Rajak checked the flight timings and informed Hussain that there is a flight at 5.00 p.m. to Nagpur. He called Hussain and said, if you hurry, we can catch the 5.00 p.m. flight and reach Nagpur today itself."

Hussain told Rajak to book the tickets immediately and be prepared for departure in another 10 minutes.

Hussain, Rajak and another team member were on the way to the airport when Hussain rechecked the instrument. It was clear that from the red star that Kasab was stationed in Nagpur.

All three of them were boarding the flight when the head steward asked for the phone to be switched off.

Hussain protested that he was expecting some important calls and will switch off the mobile before the plane started cruising.

The Security Inspector said, "I am sorry Sir, due to some special instructions today, we have been ordered to take away all phones and any other devices from the passengers and give it back at the destination.

Hussain tried to protest but the Security inspector was overpowering. He told him, "Either you deposit all the phones and smart devices, or we will download your group."

Hussain had no option but to comply.

The Inspector said, "We need the GPS which is in your bag also. Hussain switched it off and with great irritation and handed it over to the Inspector."

All three of them got into the plane. As they took their seats came the announcement that the flight was delayed by half an hour due to some weather problems.

The flight reached Nagpur at 9.00 p.m.

Hussain switched on the mobile phone the moment he got it and was relieved to see that the red star was still blinking at Nagpur.

Hussain and his companions made their way out with and got on to a taxi. Hussain told the driver to take them to the Grand hotel and it took them another half an hour to check into their rooms

Hussain again checked up the mobile instrument. The Red star seemed to be been blinking at the same point from yesterday.

Hussain decided to look up the road map and pinpoint the place. Having pin pointed the placed he sent a sms asking for a certain address. Within moments came the reply with an address.

Hussain and the team got ready. First, they went to the address given in the sms and it seemed to be a desolated area.

There was a shop called, "Peace". Hussain rang the bell and the door opened. Hussain walked in.

'Peace be with you", said Hussain to the man, who was about 70 years old with white hair and a long beard. He was dressed in white Pyjama and Kurtha covering his feet with glaring white sandals.

'Peace be with you', replied Hussain.

Hussain said, 'Zakir sent his regards'

The white dressed man was very cautious and polite.

He asked, 'which Zakir?'

'Zakir Ali from Pakistan', said Hussain.

The old man said, 'My name is Abdul Rahman'. 'Since Zakir has sent you, I am very happy to offer you tea. Please have tea. He called a boy and asked him to bring two cups of tea. The tea came immediately.

Hussain was impatient. But he knew that he can't show his impatience in this place. Hussain started to sip the tea.

Abdul Rahman took out his mobile. He typed some message and pressed the send button.

In a couple of minutes, he received a message.

Abdul Rahman seemed to be pleased with the sms and he asked of Hussain, "How can I be service to you?"

Hussain asked for three pistols with bullets.

Abdul Rahaman asked, 'You want it on Sale or for hire.'

Hussain smiled. He knew if he had said for hire, he would have been shot immediately. He said, "I will buy it."

Abdul Rahman placed "Shop Closed" sign in the entrance locked the front door and led Hussain to a door leading to another room.

Hussain choose three Black Cobras and took a case of bullets.

Abdul Rahaman asked for Rs. 85,000/- and Hussain pealed 1000-rupee notes and gave it to Abdul Rahman

"'Peace be with you'" said Abdul Rahaman.

"Peace be with you" said Hussain, knowing fully well any other reply would have also got him killed.

Abdul Rahman led him to the front door of the shop.

Hussain opened the door and went to car waiting in which his men waited.

Getting into the car, he opened the mobile and saw the red light blinking on the same spot. He activated the road map and gave the driver instructions.

After one hour of driving, they reached a hotel called 'Sweet Memories.'

The red light turned to green light.

Hussain thought for some time. The green light indicated that the target is within 150 feet.

Hussain and party entered the hotel and the receptionist greeted them, "Welcome to Sweet Memories. How can we be of help?"

Hussain with a smile which usually mesmerised most of the girls said, "We need a room for four of us."

The receptionist replied, "I am sorry Sir, no rooms are available". Can we try our branch hotel which is in the next street?"

The receptionist had been advised to redirect unknown room seekers to their branch hotel which was not doing too well.

Hussain short temper came to the fore and receptionist realized this man was different from his appearance itself. Beneath the handsome façade she felt something was not right and it sent creepers up her body. This seemed to be danger and she felt very unsure.

Recovering she felt she might as well use this situation to her advantage for extra incentive. She decided to go against the hotel order and told Hussain, "If it's ok with you, we can accommodate you in a Deluxe Suit which will cost double the cost of the normal suite."

Hussain smiling inwards said, "I will take that."

Thrilled the receptionist told him that the Suite would be Rupees ten thousand per day and inquired, "Will it be cash or credit?"

'Cash', replied Hussain.

The receptionist gave a form and asked Hussain to fill it up.

Hussain was filling up the form and came to the address box. Hussain thought of giving an Indian city address. However, he hesitated since it was clearly said that address proof was required for acceptance of the form.

So, he gave a Pakistan address given in his passport.

The receptionist went through the form and noticed the Pakistan address. This time she didn't want to ignore her basic instinct warnings.

She discreetly pressed a red button and a photograph was taken.

"'Sir, I need your Passport", asked the receptionist

Hussain who normally suppressed his anger was today barely able to control himself. He was not sure why. Realizing he coundn't afford any suspicion, quietly took his passport and gave it to the receptionist.

The receptionist took a photocopy of Hussain's passport and handed it over to Hussain.

Hussain was uneasy at this though he didn't show it outwardly.

The receptionist told the bellboy to take them to Suit No. 101.

Hussain opened the device and checked the position of the blinking star.

The star was clicking rapidly, and it meant that the target was within 100 feet.

CHAPTER

34

The Bell Boy informed well in advance, took him directly to the Manager's room.

The Manager welcomed Paul Kumar and led him to a sofa and both of them sat down. The Manager then ordered the bell boy to get them some fresh special tea.

The Managing Director handed over the copy of the passport and photograph of Hussain.

Paul Kumar had one look at the photograph and asked, 'How many people know that this Hussain is staying in this hotel?"

"Three of us, the manager, the receptionist and myself", replied the Manager.

Paul Kumar told the Manager, 'Ask the receptionist to come this room immediately."

The receptionist, a little jittery came into the room unsure of herself.

Paul Kumar asked, "What's your name?"

"Mary James" replied the receptionist.

Paul Kumar told her, "Mary, go to the counter and keep your manager informed about every moment of this Hussain. Even if he comes to tea to tea shop, it has to be reported. Do you understand?"

"Yes", said Mary and left.

Paul Kumar told the manager, "Give me a room with a computer, scanner and plenty of tea".

The room was arranged, and Paul Kumar opened the system and logged on to his email in a secure server.

He scanned Hussain's photograph and sent a mail to an address.

Paul Kumar was waiting for reply.

The reply came within five minutes, "Known Terrorist but has not committed any offence in India. Proceed with utmost caution. There will be one Taake Singh staying in the same hotel. Inform him immediately."

Paul Kumar went to Taake Singh's room and knocked the door. Taake Singh greeted him and both exchanged some regular codes.

After that Paul told Taake Singh, "There is a Pakistani named Hussain who arrived about half an hour back and has taken a suit in the hotel."

Taake Singh smiled and said, "He is following me. Please do one thing. Take this tracker and give it one of your agents. Ask him to roam around in his car for half an hour and meet me at Higginbotams book store at the airport, in one hour's time."

On a phone call from Paul, his assistant Vinod came within ten minutes. Taake Singh gave him the instructions.

Vinod left with the tracker.

Taake Singh packed his only brief case and was ready to check out.

Taake Singh told Paul, "Hussain should not know that we know anything about him, and no one should approach or arrest him. This is something to do with National security. Please ensure this."

Paul replied, "Don't worry Sir; we already have instructions from very high command to do what you told us to do. It will be adhered to."

Taake Singh said, "Another thing. Hussain will soon be asking for a self driven car. Ask the hotel to give him an Innova with just one litre of petrol in the tank. Try and delay bringing the car as much as possible. This will give me time to call my superiors and plan our next move."

CHAPTER

35

Hussain was pondering over his next move. Then he noticed that the star had started moving.

He got up in a hurry and asked one of his men to come along with him. By this time the green light had turned red.

Hussain and his man hurried to the front desk. He handed over Rs 100/- to the receptionist and with a smiling face asked the receptionist to get him a self driven car fast. The receptionist well aware of what had to be done told Hussain, "Sir, please sit down while I organize for the same and got on to the telephone. She pretended to check with one agent after another in a believable manner. After 10 minutes of waiting Hussain not able to control himself shouted at the receptionist, "is our car coming or not?"

At the same moment an Innova was bought to the entrance of hotel by a valet. The valet had ensured that only one litre of petrol was in the fuel tank. The fuel gauge had been adjusted to display that petrol was almost full.

The receptionist said, "Sorry Sir, for the delay. Currently we have no car in the hotel and took us some time to get one from the agency."

Hussain with his companion got into the car and took off in a hurry towards the direction of the star in the device.

Taake Singh called up Sunil and briefed him on what happened.

Sunil instructed Take Singh to go to Chennai in some zig zag manner and report from there.

Paul and Taake Singh went to the hotel lobby and checked out.

Takke Singh said to Paul, "Take me to the Nagpur Railway station. In another half an hour a train will leave for Chennai. I want to get into that train. Ask Vinod to meet us at Nagpur Railway Station exactly at 2.00 p.m. on Platform No.3. The train to Chennai will also start at 2pm. I want the tracker to be handed over to me exactly at 2.00 p.m."

Taake said, "Ok, now the time is 1.30 p.m. Hope you are clear in what has to be done".

'Yes Sir'

Paul phoned Vinod and gave him the instructions. Once he had conveyed the instructions, he asked, "Is Hussain still behind you in that Innova?"

Vinod replied, "No, their Innova stopped after following him for 15 minutes".

Everything went on as planned by Taake Singh.

They went to Nagpur Station at 1.55 p.m and reached Platform No.3.

Taake Singh's mobile rang, it was Sunil Singh. Sunil warned that under no circumstances should Hussain be arrested nor should become aware that the person carrying the mobile is not Kasab. Inform this to Nagpur agent Paul Kumar and take utmost care". He further said, "Till now you have done a great job"

Taake Singh replied, 'Yes Sir', thrilled at an appreciation coming from a person so senior as Sunil who was believed to be close to even the Prime Minister."

Vinod came exactly at two pm and handed over the tracker to Takke Singh.

Hussain was in rage. His entire face had become red and he seemed to breath our sheer fire. They were standing in the middle of the road and trying to desperately wave down a taxi.

Hussain checked his navigator to find the red star had started moving. A taxi cab pulled over and all the three got into the car. Husssain directed the driver to take them to Sweet Memories Hotel.

They arrived at the hotel and went to the reception. Hussain threw the key at the receptionist and told her that she should have had some idiotic sense to provide her clients with a car that was not equipped to go long distance. As the key hit the receptionist, he shouted," Keep the bill ready by the time we come down. We don't want to stay in hotel which provides shabby service".

He decided to wait for the star to stop at some place after which he will track down the same and finish off Kasab.

CHAPTER

36

The leader said, "If you make any attempt to escape or create problems, we will kill all three of you. So, behave yourself."

Vijaykar understood. Even though he was a 3 Dan black belt in Karate, he had no hope of taking on the ten well built persons, who were also armed.

All three of them were bundled out of the station into a Sumo and the vehicles started to move at high speed towards a mountainous terrain.

The cars raced into suburbs of hilly region and entered a jungle. Vijaykar was observing all this constantly, trying to evaluate the chances of an escape.

After four hours of journey, it was dawn. They reached a mountain. They were asked to get out and then motioned to start to get on to horses waiting for them. Vijaykar got on to one horse and asked Rani to hand him the boy which he settled in front of him. Then he asked her to get up at the back and hold him. Rani felt uncomfortable but did as Vijaykar asked her to do. It surprised her that once she slipped her arms around Vijaykar, she felt very comfortable. Raj Kiran also felt nice nestled between Vijaykar's thighs and body which seemed to protect him and found it exciting as the horse started trotting.

After two hours of climbing their way up, they were asked to get down from their horse and move in a straight line. They obeyed the orders left with no choice.

One of them said, "Get moving".

During the climb, Vijaykar heard cries of wild animals. Roars of lions were frequent, and they could see wild elephants now and then. They finally reached a wooden bridge which they crossed and came into a pathway covered by huge boulders on each side. They moved through the path and after a walk of about 15 minutes reached a village.

Then the leader turned to Vijaykar and said, don't try to escape. You will be free to do what you want here in this village. But keep in mind that if even one of you go missing, we will hold the tribals responsible and make their life miserable. They understand our language well.

He continued, "They realize that unless they obey us, they aren't safe."

After giving some instruction to the Chief of the tribe, the terrorists left the captives on top village under the guard of the tribals.

A hut was given to the three of them to stay in.

Vijaykar and Rani having nothing else to do found solace in each other's presence and interacted well. The got to know each other well and felt nice in each others presence. Rani was overwhelmed with Vijaykar's personality and for the first time, felt herself being intensely attracted to someone.

Over their conversation the also learnt from the boy that he was the grandson of the Prime Minister.

Their conversation was suddenly interrupted when a wild scream came from one of the huts.

CHAPTER

37

Arjun, Sunil, Rita and Zarina reached Gangtok and checked into a grand hotel through special arrangements made by the PM' Office.

Upon checking in, they all gathered together at an open-air restaurant for a cup of tea. The tea was supplied by a young tribal.

Sunil announced, "Arjun and me, will do a trip to check the mountains."

He further said we already have our kit ready for action. The kit consisted of sub machine guns, close range automatic self-loading rifles, small pistols, nerve gas grenades and other necessary equipments required for a mission of this sort.

Always ready for adventure Zarina inquired, "can we also join you?"

Sunil's response was immediate. Let's not take too much risk. I suggest you get some rest.

Rita agreed and with Zarina in her tow, walked over to the terrace over looking the entrance to the hotel. As they built up a conversation Zarina inquired of Rita if she was in love with Arjun. The question jolted Rita. It was not because Zarina has asked the question, but it made her wonder if she had compromised her organization in any manner.

Zarina said, "It doesn't take much for a female to understand body language of another female especially with such a handsome guy like Arjun around."

Something caught Rita's attention. She asked Zarina, "Whether she had also seen the same Maruti Omni parked outside, when they came in?"

Zarina said, "Yes. It's very much the same. But what brings your attention to the same."

Rita said, "I thought I saw a glint of a binocular lens and feel they are watching us ". At the same moment the Zarina saw something move and a light seemingly from a lens caught her attention as well.

Both agreed to remain casual and continue their conversation while keeping a watch on the van and settled themselves in a table which gave them ample coverage.

Sunil and Arjun readied themselves with their gear and went down to the reception and got into the jeep reserved for them.

As Arjun drove the jeep out of the hotel's entrance, the presence of the parked maruti van disturbed him. He was about to turn back when Sunil advised him, "Don't do that." Drive straight down and lets hope the security that's been arranged by the P.M.'s Office is good enough to protect Zarina and Rita.

Arjun asked for directions from some locals on the way and headed towards the mountains. They were climbing a narrow pathway in the mountain when the same Maruti over took them.

The pathway was steep with number of bends and u turns. As they approached one of the signals which indicated a U turn, Arjun noticed a car coming behind them. He felt, maybe it was some adventurous tourist.

As they took the curve ahead, Arjun had to slam the brakes to avoid hitting the body of a person lying in a pool of blood and in the process veered to the left and almost hit the boulder. Sunil followed by Arjun got down from the car and ran towards the body when two men appeared with gun in their hand from behind the boulders which had hidden them.

It was clear that it was an ambush. Realising their position both Sunil and Arjun lifted their arms and surrendered to the situation.

It took all of them by a surprise when a Qualis car came around the bend and ran over the body on the ground and crashed into the Maruti Van from behind. The impact made the van move forward and hit the men who had come from the boulder and burst into a whole ball of flame.

———————◄◆►———————

CHAPTER

38

Both Vijaykar and Rani rushed towards the big hut where the screaming emanated from.

There were tribal men standing at the entrance of the hut. The chief of the village with a worried look was standing in a very troubled manner.

"Haka boko, Haka booka boo" barked the chief at Vijaykar and Rani as they made their way into the hut.

Vijaykar was puzzled. One of the tribal seeing the confusion on Vijaykar's face, gesticulated by swinging his arms with something in it.

Rani realized that a child birth was in process and went into the hut. Something was clearly wrong with the baby. It had not come down but the intense pain which the mother was suffering from was apparent. As she looked into the vagina, she realized that this was a classic case in which if a caesarean is not performed the baby and the mother would die.

All the doctor instincts came to the fore and she went out immediately and explained the situation to Vijaykar. It was when she was explaining to Vijaykar that she realized a complete Medical kit had been with her in the car when she was kidnapped. This she had seen at the hut which was given to them.

Rani pulling Vijaykar told him, "Please bring over my medical kit which is kept in my baggage in our hut."

A surprised Vijakar ran to the hut and brought the medical kit. Rani asked him to try and get her some boiling water as soon as possible.

After handing over the medical kit to Rani, poor Vijaykar tried his best but remained unsuccessful in getting the tribals to get him a pot full of hot water.

Then suddenly one of the tribal who had just entered asked, "I know English, tell me, what you want?"

Vijaykar was surprised and told him that he needs good boiling water in a pot immediately to be sent to the hut.

The tribal said something to the chief in their local language and immediately a fire was set up and water was boiled in tribal earthenware.

Rani came out and took the boiling water and after half an hour of tense moments, Rani came out holding a new born baby. Everyone jumped with joy.

Rani explained to Vijaykar, "It seems to be the grandson of the chief. "

Amidst all these actions, a tiger had entered into the village and with a roar it pounced on a lad and started dragging him away into the jungle. The tribal men folk ran to get their spears and attack the tiger.

Vijaykar, realizing the danger of few more moments of inaction, grabbed a hunting knife and sprinted and plunged the knife deep into its back and whipped out the knife. Releasing the lad, the tiger turned around viciously to attack. Vijaykar plunged the knife into one of the eyes of the tiger and blood started gushing out. Unable to bear the pain, the tiger with a shrieking cry, dropped the lad and sprinted back into the forest.

As the lad got up and came towards Vijaykar, all tribals fell on their knees and bowed to Vijayakar, hooting, "Godhoo, Godhoo."

The tribal who knew English explained, "They are thanking you as a God decent and you can be assured, they would do anything to help you when required."

The lad happened to be the youngest son of the Chief's third wife.

The chief came and hugged Vijaykar.

Then to his command, a local brew was brought and offered to Vijaykar and Rani. It seemed to be a typical village celebration with the bonfire in the middle and soon everyone was inebriated and dancing around the fire. Vijaykar and Rani were also dragged into the celebration and they too enjoyed themselves inebriated by the local brew.

The celebrations came to an abrupt halt after half and hour, when two tribals standing guard near the edge of the village, ran to the chief and said something. The celebration mood immediately ended, and the village folks seemed to be extremely frightened.

Vijakar caught hold of the tribal who knew English and asked him his name. The tribal replied, "Billoo."

Vijaykar asked of him, "Why are your people so tense?"

Biloo replied, "A group of men armed with different kinds of weapons were coming towards the village. As a practice they come and rape our girls after drinking our brew which they are very fond of. We are helpless against the sophisticated weapons they have."

Vijaykar told Biloo that he will help them against the cruel men and asked whether his people would listen to him.

After asking the permission of the Chief, Biloo told Vijaykar that they saw no harm in listening to him since they had nothing to lose.

Vijakar told Billoo to check and tell him how many people were coming?

Five replied Billoo after checking up.

Vijaykar inquired of Billoo whether they had any jungle poison which can kill a man immediately.

Billoo himself replied they have lot of poisonous snake venoms that could do the job.

Vijaykar told Billoo of a plan which he translated to the Chief.

As per Vijaykar's advise, all the tribals were sent to their huts and told to remain silent.

The Chief gestured 10 tribal fighters to do what was said by Vijaykar through Biloo and they nodded their agreement.

Vijaykar ordered the tribals to make five mounds of hay stacks in the open centre of the village and asked two tribals with Bow and arrow smeared with the poison, to hide in each of the stacks.

As planned the Chief pretended to do something at the centre of the open space in the village surrounded by five stacks of hay. He was holding a torch and looked to be praying to the sky. The five terrorists made their way into the circle of hay stacks and were curious of something new being done by the Chief.

They were happy to see their favourite brew kept in front of the hay stacks in pots. They went and sat next to it and started drinking it watching the Chief doing something for half an hour. By the time the men had fully finished brew in the pots and they were inebriated with the brew they had drunk.

Then one of them kicked the Chief to open his eyes and asked him, "Where are the prisoners?" The Chief replied, "In that hut", and tried to get back to his act of praying by motioning them to go and check for themselves.

One of the men laughed and said, "Oh chief, we believe you since you don't have any other choice. Now lead us to the hut where your good girls are assembled. I believe you daughter looks very good. Bring her also to us. "

The chief bowed down with uncontrollable anger and did what he had never done earlier i.e. take on the offenders by giving the previously agreed signal.

The tribals hiding inside in each of the hay stack released their arrows on the men sitting in an inebriated state with deadly precision. The inebriated terrorists died instantly.

The chief called Billoo and spoke to him for a long time and gestured at Vijaykar.

Billo came to Vijakar and said, "The chief is now afraid that the once the terrorist realize that these five have not returned, will send a force to come here and destroy us."

Vijaykar asked, "When do they usually come to this village and how long they stay here?"

Biloo replied, "The come once in 7 days to keep an eye on what we are doing. They stay for a few days and return when we have brewed enough of our local stuff and take it away."

Vijaykar said, "So, these men will not be missed for some time"

Biloo said, "No."

Vijaykar through Billoo told their Chief to burry all the bodies and keep their weapons safe somewhere.

The Chief sent some orders and the men got working to do the necessary.

Vijaykar went to the wooden bridge they had to cross on their way to this place and observed the surrounding all around.

Vijaykar asked of Biloo, "Is that wooden bridge the only way to this place."

Billoo replied, "Yes."

Vijaykar asked, "Then why don't you destroy the bridge to keep the terrorist away?"

Billoo replied, "If we do that, we cannot go down ever. We will be cut off from our farming and hunting requirements. So, it's our interest to protect the bridge at all cost since it means so much to our existence. He added it's lucky that these men don't know about this. They have warned us that if we destroy the bridge, they will send in metal birds and wipe us out.

Vijaykar impressed on the Chief that, "these men were terrorist working against India and were illegally occupying this place. He then said, soon people will come looking for the three of them brought in by the terrorist and their hideout down in these hills will be located and wiped out. Until then we have to defend ourselves."

Then, Vijaykar asked the Chief, "Any idea, how many terrorists are at the base camp?"

The Chief replied," About 150 to 200."

Vijaykar asked Billoo to check with his Chief, "How many men in your tribe can fight?"

On the Chief's reply, Billoo told Vijaykar that all of them would do whatever is required to fight these terrible people."

Just then Rani appeared.

Vijakar asked Rani, "How is the little boy doing?"

Rani replied, "He seems to be making friends with tribal children and has started playing around with the snakes which frightens me."

"What! playing with snakes", exclaimed Vijaykar.

"Yes, they were playing with mountain snakes each about 10 feet long"

Then Vijaykar asked of the Chief through Biloo, "is it usual for your children play with snakes?"

The chief replied "Oh they are harmless and there are hundreds of them. The kids love and play with them whenever they are free. So we remove the poison which is stored for medicinal purposes and give the children the harmless snakes to play with. He added, from what we have seen, the snakes also love the children and play with them".

Vijaykar enquired, "How do the terrorist feel about the snakes."

Both the Chief and Billo chuckled, "They are dead scared of snakes for some reason."

Vijaykar then through Biloo explained a plan to the Chief as to how they can defend themselves from these evil people.

Vijaykar then inquired, "How long will it take, to get some snake pits made on the boulder adjoining the path way leading to the bridge."

The reply came, "don't worry; we will get it done in a day's time."

Vijaykar reminded them, "don't forget to get the poisoned arrows prepared as well."

The Chief laughed and said, "That will also be ready, when ever required."

CHAPTER

39

A smiling Rita and Zarina removed their Burka's and got down from the Qualis car.

Arjun questioned Rita "how on the earth did you get here?"

Rita replied, "We simply followed you." She explained him that on seeing the maruti van took after Arjun and Sunil, they decided to follow and check out the situation.

Arjun was about to say something when Rita inquired to him," Well did you locate the mountain or not?"

Arjun managed to blurt out, "Well we were on our way."

Rita enjoying herself told, "I know the mountain you are looking for."

"Really", said Arjun."

Rita said," not only I know it's whereabouts, but I have also located a person who is willing to take us there."

Us! Stop this nonsense. It's no place for ladies, "Arjun said in a stern voice."

Rita mockingly told him, "Well, when we can save you from being ambushed, we know how to take care of ourselves too."

A fuming Arjun was about to say something when Sunil laughingly put his arm around Arjun and said, "Aare, "let them also come. We seem to be in this all together."

Arjun inquired of Rita, "How come you located a guide who can take us there."

Rita enjoying herself said, "The tea boy, you remember"

Arjun and Sunil Singh were surprised.

Rita asked, "Do you remember a tribal serving you tea?"

Sunil Singh said "Yes."

Rita said, "He is the person who will take us to the mountain top. He is from the same tribe living on the top of the mountain."

Sunil Singh suddenly realized that they are talking in the middle of the road and vulnerable to an attack.

Sunil Singh said, "Let us move away from here and go to the hotel and discuss our plants."

All of them got into the Toyota Qualis car and went to their hotel.

CHAPTER

40

Sunil Singh, Arjun, Rita, Zenaat and the five commandos, assembled inside Sunil's room. The bed was moved aside and the table dragged to the centre to enable them sit and confer.

Rita smiling to herself, dialled some number from her mobile and ordered for tea. The tea was served by the tribal who had earlier served in the morning.

The tribal smiled at Rita. Rita said, "Hi Hota, how are you?"

Hota the tribal seemed to be mesmerised with by Rita. He beamed and said, "Very well madam".

Arjun felt very irritated the way Hota was looking at Rita. Rita showed Hota a map and asked, "Hota, will you take us to this mountain?"

Hota said, "Madam, like I said told you yesterday, we will all get killed. I don't want Memsahib to die". There are very evil people out there. I escaped somehow and came to this city. That's why, even though I want to get back and live with my tribe, I am working in this hotel."

Sunil Singh told Hota, "Don't be afraid, we have got guns and showed him his pistol."

Hota laughed and said, "Those evil people have bigger guns then yours."

Sunil Singh said, "Don't worry, we too have bigger guns."

Hota said, "Those evil people come to this town once a week to buy provisions. You look at them yourself and then you will understand."

All of them were surprised. Arjun asked, "How will they be dressed?"

Hota replied, "They dress like ordinary tourists to ensure they are not seen as some one different."

Sunil Singh asked, "How come then you recognise them?"

Hota replied, "As I told you I was in the mountain village. All my brothers and sisters are in the village which is in the top of mountain. And I have seen them there."

Sunil Singh asked Hota, "then, how come you are here?"

Hota said, "Well I ran away."

Sunil asked, "Hota, can you tell us why you ran away from your people, brothers and sisters."

Very mournfully, Hota told them, "One day, two of those evil people came dragged my beautiful wife and raped her. They took her into the forest away from our village and then did things which I don't want to talk about."

Where were you, "asked, Sunil Singh?"

Hota went on, "I was hiding behind a tree watching them. After some time, they started torturing here asking some funny questions which I couldn't hear. I could not bear it any longer and so I ran and plunged my spear in to one of them killing him instantly. The other took out an automatic pistol and started shooting at me. My brave wife took the opportunity to grab a heavy stone and crashed it on his head from behind. Blood came gashing out. Then she took the spear from other terrorist threw it on the terrorist who suddenly came in to view.

It struck his belly, but the terrorist shot my wife and she passed out. I could hear some sound and quickly hid in a bush. Hearing the shots few of the terrorist colleagues came running to the spot where the bodies were lying. Then one of them saw my foot prints which pointed to the bush I was hiding in. Fearful of getting caught, I got up and ran for my life.

"How did you get away?" asked Arjun."

The mountain is place where we have grown up playing hide and seek. I know the mountain inside out. Well at least the part I have frequented often. I ran with minimum effort and made the terrorist run in circles. They separated to trap me. Actually, they were landing into my trap. I led them to path which leads to a quick sand. Two of them fell in the quick sand and I watched with great glee.

Then one of the terrorists came and tried to help the terrorist sinking in the quick sand. I crept behind and killed him with my spear. Before the fourth terrorist could reach me, I ran for my life down the hills since that was the only way left. I finally reached here and to keep myself alive, I started serving tea in a small tea shop. Slowly I learned a bit of language and then this hotel employed me.

Rita gave Hota a nice smile and said, "If you take us to the mountain, we can help release your people from the terrorist clutches."

A blushing Hota, did not know what to say. Then he said, "I am afraid they will kill me the moment they see me. They have got a photograph of me which one of them took out of their mobile phone."

Rita to Arjun's irritation patted Hota on his back and said, "Whether you take us or not we will be going anyway. Think about it tonight and let us know tomorrow."

Hota bowed down in a tribal manner and went of the room.

Realising the anxiety in Sunil and Arjun's face, Rita said, "Don't worry, I will make him to take us to the mountain." They retreated to their rooms.

CHAPTER

41

Hota was on his way was wondering what to do? On one hand, he didn't know how to tell the lovely madam, no. He even wondered why and realized there was something in her which displaced his mind.

But altogether, it was nice feeling and enjoying it; he headed for the tea shop. Sipping his tea, so lost was he in his thoughts, that he didn't notice his friend Bota joining him at the table.

Looking at Hota's lost face, Bota inquired, "What are you thinking about and added, looks like you are thinking of marrying again?"

A badly embarrassed Hota tried his best to hide his feelings which he felt had betrayed him. He told Bota, "Enough, don't joke. You know how much I loved my wife and what agony I have been through since I lost her?"

Bota enquired, "Then what is that has taken you into thoughts of such high priority that you didn't even notice me."

Bota and Hota were close friends. They talked about everything on earth.

Hota said, "I have come across a group of people who wants me to take them to the mountains."

Bota asked, "What for? Have you told them that the mountains are controlled by rapists and murderers?"

"Yes. I told them. Moreover, there is a beautiful Madam there whom I like and I don't want anything to happen to her," replied Hota.

Ha Ha Ha, laughed Bota and said, "So I wasn't wrong in my guess on seeing the expression on your face."

Hota was silent. Bota was Hota's wife's cousin. There was an uneasy silence between them.

Bota loved Hota and decided to get over this impasse. He looked at Hota and told him, "if these people will help us to kill some of the terrorist, I don't mind taking them to the mountains, even if means risking my life."

Knowing Bota hated those terrorists, despite his fear for them, Hota replied, "I am sure there is going to be a fight there with the terrorist. These people also have weapons like those terrorists, and they are definitely planning to find the mountain whether we take them or not."

Bota replied, "We should definitely take them there then. At least we can have some of those shaitans killed."

Hota inquired, "Will you come with me and talk to them tomorrow?"

Bota said, "I will definitely come".

He continued, "I have an ace up my sleeve. I know of a secret way to go to our village entirely different from the normal track."

Hota exclaimed! "What, you have never mentioned this to me till date. Since when you have started hiding things from me?"

Bota replied, "Come on. Don't forget that whenever I tried to talk to you about the mountains, you got up and went away. I had no opportunity to tell you my discovery."

Hota inquired of Bota, "How did you discover this secret route?"

A slightly uneasy Bota told Hota, "He will only tell him on his promise that he wont ever leak this secret to anyone."

On Hota's promise, Bota continued, "Do you remember the old ruined castle built by Kings long ago?"

"Yes", said Hota.

Bota started, "There is a secret tunnel from the castle all the way up to our village. It goes all the way to that funny dungeon in the castle from where at times you could hear ghost like noise. It was considered haunted by evils and all were forbidden to go anywhere near it.

One day before my marriage, I had taken that earlier girl friend of mine to the spot and we were having fun. Unfortunately, her father had come hunting that side and hearing his daughter's voice, he made his way towards us.

Both of us were very scared and she pretended to be playing with some pebbles. I knew I had move away from the scene without being seen to avoid any disgrace to my girl friend. The only place I could escape was by ducking into the dungeon. I was very frightened but decided that even death was better than getting my poor girl friend from being disgraced.

I scrambled to the dungeon and fell into a pit. It was suffocating. Hiding in silence, I realized that the noise that was being spoken about came only when a draft of fresh air came which helped my breathing. I got curious and went in to check it further, when I came across the tunnel. I felt that maybe it's the breeze through the tunnel that was making the noise and lost my fear.

Since I had nothing to do for some time, I decided to explore the tunnel further. After almost 5 hours by which I was exhausted, I came to the end and found an opening which was shielded by a very thick bush. Coming out of the bush I realized and that it was the second base of the mountain. It was a huge short cut too. I made my way up to ensure my absence is not spotted and managed to get into my hut just before sunrise.

I never had an opportunity to tell it to anyone else but for the first time I realized I had a secret which might make me famous in the tribe and help me get married to the tribal Chief's beautiful daughter, which was my childhood dream."

A little upset Hota inquired, "So how come you did not reveal your surprise to become famous and marry the Chief's daughter?"

Bota replied, "I was planning to do so, till, my parents fixed up with your parents and informed me that you are going to be married to Hota's sister and made me meet up with her. I was very sceptical and just met your sister for the sake of it. Interacting with the angel of your sister, I realized that I had to look no further and happily nodded my acceptance to my parents. Rest is history. You know. Maybe now you will realize how deep I was in my love with your sister."

Hota was moved. He hugged Bota.

Bota said, "It's pretty late. Let's meet with your people in the morning, let's go to our rooms and get some rest."

Both met early in the morning at the same tea shop. Bota also worked in the same hotel as a cleaner in the kitchen.

At an agreed time, both were standing in front of Room number No, 707.

Hota, knocked.

Sunil was sitting brooding over some message. Hearing the knock, he peeped through the peep hole and on seeing Hota and another similar looking lad; he quickly opened the door and motioned them to get into the room immediately.

As Sunil closed the door, Hota said, "Sir, this is Bota my cousin."

Sunil Singh seeing his tea was over called up room service to send them another four cups of tea.

Arjun came out from the bathroom and gesticulated to Sunil, "who is this new addition with Hota?"

Hota introduced Bota to Arjun and Sunil as his brother-in-law, who also wanted to get involved, if decision had to be taken on going to the mountains.

Sunil remarked, "So Bota is aware of our yesterday's conversation?" "Yes", replied Hota.

By the time a server who came to server the tea seemed surprised to see Hota and Bota in the room. But he didn't say anything and left.

There was another knock on the door.

As usual, the fully prepared Sunil peeped through the door to find Rita and Zarina standing in front.

He opened the door and said, "Please come in. Hota has just walked in with his brother-in-law Bota. He made it very clear that they both always take joint decisions and therefore he had brought him as well."

From the expression on Sunil's face, neither Rita nor Zarina felt it right to question him and came into the room and sat down.

Hota, not bothered about others, addressed Rita "Madam, this is my cousin who knows the mountain like the back of his hand. He has agreed to help us take you the mountain provided some of his queries are clarified."

Rita looked up to Sunil who nodded his agreement.

Bota directly asked Sunil Singh, "Why are you going to the mountain Sir? It is a very dangerous place."

Sunil Singh, who was also highly qualified psychologist, realized that these naïve tribals had decided to support them from their way of questioning. He realized that he could either tell them the truth or spin some story. But then also felt that, if Bota came to know he had spun a story, he might not cooperate at a crucial stage and felt truth would be the best way out."

He replied, "We want to rescue some people known to us who have been kidnapped by the terrorist and taken to the hills."

Bota questioned, "Can we know who is being held there whom you want to so desperately rescue?"

Sunil Singh realized that, Bota, a wise person by instinct, didn't appear to be a shrewd negotiator. He addressed him in a very stern voice, "Enough of your questioning. We will let you know the full truth if you promise to help us. Apart from that we will also arrange to provide you with a good amount of money which will help in building of your village. He, acting in the role of an agitated person said, you can either take it or leave it."

Hota and Bota looked at each other.

Bota said in a subtle voice, "Sir we are not doing it for money. We have our own reason to kill all those evil people who are causing hell to our tribe".

The honest appeal from Bota was apparent to Sunil.

He asked of Bota, "Very well, when can we start?"

Bota said, "Give me little time. I will come back to you with a plan."

Bota and Hota left and made their way to their accommodation.

CHAPTER

42

Bota and Hota were having tea in the evening at the same tea shop. Bota surprised Hota by suddenly saying, I have got very good relationship with the chief of the Bottom village.

"How come?" asked Hota.

Bota said, "Well. I am due to marry the daughter of the Chief of bottom village," soon.

Rascal, shouted Hota, "how come you have never told me."

Bota said, "I got approval only last night".

He continued, "The only problem is that the Chief is afraid that the terrorists will kill me if they see me. So, he has advised me to plan for an accommodation down here where there will be no such danger. Once I have made the arrangements, I will get married and bring her down here."

Hota said, "You are talking as if these terrorists don't come down here and keep a check as well?"

Bota said, "That's why I would like to do anything to destroy the terrorist and free our people from their clutches.

He continued. "After talking to your group last night, I feel that the right time has come. The people whom we spoke, has their objective and will do anything to achieve that. If we do the right thing and utilize them, I think we can achieve our objective as well."

Hota, not knowing how to respond said, "lets forget all this for now and rejoice the news of your engagement with the, "Bottom Mountain Chief's daughter".

Both Hota and Bota always loved drinks. They made their way to a highway bar and sat down to drink."

Both were feeling nice enjoying their drinks and food when one new face appeared and gauged the atmosphere from the entrance. On convincing himself that this place looked safe, he gave a sign and entered another four bearded persons. They took their seats, opposite to table in which Hota and Bota were seated.

They ordered for some drinks and started drinking. Initially they didn't talk much but kept drinking. As the drinks had their effect, they started talking.

Their conversation was audible to both Hota and Bota. The language was Urdu. But both Hota and Bota exposed to various languages in the hotel were able to understand what they were talking.

The red bearded one said," Our commander is in a very good mood. He wants to establish a base in this town."

The second bearded man asked, "What for?"

The red bearded one said, "For establishing a communication centre".

"What about the one we are having in the mountains?" asked the third person.

The red bearded one said,"it seems that sometimes, the signals are not clear making it very difficult for communication." Therefore, they have asked to try and establish a centre in this village."

The second person asked? "Who are those people, we recently took to the tribe in the mountain top?"

The red beard got angry and said, "Fool, don't talk about that subject. How many times I have told you not talk about that matter in public."

He looked around to see whether anybody was showing interest in their conversation and noticed both Hota and Bota.

The Red beard's face became cloudy. He remarked, "I seem to have seen this chap sitting opposite to our table and added, but I am not sure where."

The remark frightened both Hota and Bota.

The second bearded said, "Oh, all these tribal people look alike. Don't rake your brain for nothing."

Both Hota and Bota felt insecure. They both quickly finished their drinks and food and after paying the bill, moved towards the entrance of the Bar. Sensing the tension in Hota, Bota advised him in a low voice, "don't move fast or slow. Walk at a normal pace, just as the way we would get out normally."

The red beard said to his friends "Let us at least question the one's face I find familiar. Another of the bearded persons who seemed to have more interest in the liquor said, "Let us not imagine and do what we have come here for. Let's enjoy this small liberty."

By the time Hota and Bhota had reached the entrance. The red beard most cautious of the lot was feeling uneasy in letting the two walks away. He got up and shouted, "STOP".

Bota took Hota by hand and whisked him away into the alley that leads to dense forest area which was familiar to both.

The four bearded men came out and but was not able to find them. The second bearded told others, "let us not expose ourselves as non tourist, and behave normally. "

All of them went back to the bar.

Terrified, both Hota and Bota decided to go and see the group in the hotel immediately. They used the fire escape to reach the floor on which Sunil and Arjun had their room and knocked on it.

CHAPTER

43

Vijaykar elaborated a plan to the Chief and seemed to be winning his confidence. Explaining in detail, he told the Chief that, it's only a matter of time before which the Govt. Officials will find a way to eradicate these terrorists invading our land. He further impressed on the Chief that; the whole of India was trying to ascertain their safe release."

Judging the effect, he seemed to have on the Chief, Vijaykar continued, "we have to defend ourselves till the police forces find a way to identify and penetrate the terrorists hold in the hills and liberate everyone. "

Examining the guns and bullets recovered from the 5 terrorists Vijyakar realized that they had 5 automatic rifles which could be used to defend themselves, Vijaykar inquired of the Chief, "how many if any of their people know how to use the rifles?"

The chief replied that they had never even seen these rifles at close range and so had no idea how to use them. Rani surprised Vijaykar by saying, "I can shoot well". Vijaykar queried, "how come?"

Rani replied, "Well, was trained to shoot during my NCC voluntary service and later in the rifle club which my father frequented".
Vijaykar said, "that makes it two of us who can operate the guns."

CHAPTER

44

Sunil Singh and Arjun were deep asleep.

Sunil Singh was having a nightmare. "He was witnessing the murder of his sister and sister's children and sad that he possibly was the reason for the incident. He was in a room and watching the murderers from a window".

Arjun woke up hearing the repeated banging on their door. He turned towards Sunil who seemed to be in a troubled sleep and as the banging started Sunil started shouting, "don't! Don't!" In his dream he was telling the terrorist to stop the shooting.

Arjun quickly went to Sunil and shook him saying "Sunil, Sunil, wake up, you are having a nightmare." Arjun then realized that it was the repeated banging on the floor which had woken him and not Sunil.

Drawing his pistol, he carefully opened the door to find Hota and Bota standing outside. Both seemed to be terribly frightened.

Arjun checked whether any body else was in the corridor and finding no one motioned both to come in.

After making them sit in comfort Arjun inquired of them" What has frightened you so badly that brings you here in the middle of the night."

Bota said, "Those people from the mountains are here in the city Sahib." By the time Sunil Singh came out of the bathroom washing his face.

Arjun asked, "What do you mean?"

"The terrorists are in the bar and one of them almost seemed to recognize me." When they headed towards us, we took to our heels", said Hota.

"Are you sure that you have not been followed here" asked Sunil Singh. "No Sahib, "We went to forest and took an unknown path to hotel."

"We are very frightened and felt that we should keep you informed", said Bota. Arjun said, "Lie down in our room, we will see what we can do in the morning."

"No Sahib, we will go our quarters in the hotel, and come here early in the morning", said Hota.

"Ok" said Arjun.

Hota and Bhota left for their quarters. As they were stepping out, Arjun said, "One more thing, be fully equipped for the journey to the mountains. We will leave sharp at 5.15 AM."

"Yes Sir", replied Hota.

CHAPTER

45

Arjun and Sunil Singh woke up at 4.00 a.m.

Arjun said, "Let us order for some tea"

Sunil phoned room service and said, "I am speaking from Room No.707. Bring us two cups of tea, please."

Next, Arjun dialled Rita's room.

Rita attended the phone call at the first ring. "

Arjun said "Good morning Sweet heart, both of you come to our room at 5.00 a.m. and be equipped for the journey to the mountains. We will be leaving by 5.30 a.m. "

Next, Arjun phoned the commandos and asked them to come to Sunil's room at 5.15 a.m.

Both Arjun and Sunil, Singh had a bath and slipped on the military camaflougiing outfits.

They took out the big box containing weapons which were available in the closet.

The weapons including silenced pistols, smoke bombs and hunting knives and two pairs of Ninchako.

Arjun told a surprised Sunil, "Well One for me and the other is for Rita. They are deadly fighting weapons in unarmed combat. Rita and I are masters in using this weapon."

First came Rita and Zarina at 5.10 a.m. Both were dressed in military uniforms.

Next came the commandos dressed similarly. Arjun distributed the weapons to the commandos, Sunil Singh, Zarina and Rita.

Rita saw the nunchako. She immediately took the weapon and tried it out and was pleased. Sunil Singh and the commandos were impressed and realized that the weapon could be deadly in close body combat.

Then Arjun took two hunting knives which were very sharp and gave it to Hota and Bota.

Seeing that, Arjun said, "I almost forgot and took out 20 star shaped gleaming things."

Sunil Singh asked, "What are these? It looks like you brought something straight out of Kung Fu movie."

Arjun answered, "They are specialized martial arts weapons," You can kill a man 15 feet away by just throwing it a certain manner" in which Rita is a specialist.

Rita put all the stars into her pocket.

At 5.45am the group started in two Hummers. After driving for about three hours they reached the border of the forest.

Here they took the cars to a deep bush and covered them with branches and leaves, to ensure that they were not visible.

Hota said, "Now we have to travel by foot Sahib".

"How long will it take?" asked Sunil.

"It will take four hours for us to reach the lower village from here. Then we have to talk to Chief and explain how you have come to get rid of the terrorist. Once plan is made, using Bota's secret route we can go the top village", replied Hota.

Sunil enquired, "Any chance of bumping into the terrorists."

"It will be difficult to predict. If the terrorists want something from Gangtok, they will come down the mountain. We have to be alert all the times", replied Hota.

They were walking for two hours, and suddenly they heard a wild laughter and saw a tribal was coming in a comical fashion.

He came to the group, and hugged Bota. Then crying out loudly he said "Brother, Brother they have rapped and killed my wife yesterday.

Sunil Singh asked Bhota, "Who is he and what has happened to him?"

Bota said, "His wife was raped before his eyes and killed." From that moment he lost his senses. He is being like that for the past two years. He has lost count of time. For him, the murder happened yesterday."

"Brother, Brother, let us go and kill all those terrorists, I want revenge", cried the tribal

Sunil Singh was worried. He asked of Bota, "Will this man's shouting attract the terrorist's attention?"

Bota replied, "They have given up on him. They have realized that his raving is normal and harmless. So, they don't even take notice of him or his ravings. He is left alone because some of the terrorist use him for their pleasure as well. "

They reached the village around 7pm. It was pitch dark.

Hota and Bohta asked the group to wait in the border of the village and said, ""Hota and myself will go and meet the chief and brief him." Then I will come and take you to the Chief. If not, they might think us as thieves and start attacking us."

"Ok", said Sunil Singh.

Hota and Bhota came running, "The militants about 50 in numbers are coming down and likely to reach the village in another two hours. The Chief wants to meet you people immediately." All of them went to the chief's hut and introductions were made.

Sunil Sing asked the chief "Have you ever resisted the terrorists in the past"

"No," said the chief. "Most of the time they come with weapons and take away the women, food and anything can they can lay their hands on"

Sunil Singh asked "Can you tell me the number of terrorists living in the mountain and where exactly are there hideouts. Also, can their hideouts be identified from air?"

The Chief said, "150 to 200 terrorists based midway between the top and bottom village. Their location unfortunately cannot be seen from air". Sunil thought for a moment and asked about the directions in which the terrorists could run if attacked.

The Chief explained, "In this particular section of the mountain they are confined to only five kilometres on either side. He said the beyond that the deep ravines block the way. Everyone knows it would be suicidal to try any other route. If they are attacked, they are likely to either go up or come down, he said."

Looking at the deep frown in Sunil's face, the Chief asked, "What's the matter".

Sunil said, "If their hideouts can be identified from air, we can bomb them using our metal birds. But the problem is that they cannot be identified from the air".

The Chief said, "If your mobile birds can spot smoke rising, we can create smoke over and below the terrorist hide outs."

Wonder struck by this simple idea from the Chief, Sunil took over and started detailing a plan, "Arjun, Rita with Hota and Bota will leave immediately for the top village. Sunil, Zarina and the commandos will hide in the village huts. Soon as Arjun & party reach the top village and secure the captives safety, Arjun would inform Sunil over a special high-powered walkie talkie. Handing over a special instrument Sunil told Arjun to also relay him the location coordinates. Sunil will then through his transmitter provide the location details of the top village and inform the air force base to drop a battalion of armed commandos both in the top and bottom village, at an appropriate time.

He said by this action a great number the terrorist will get wiped out. The ones lucky enough to escape will make their way either to the top or bottom.

The battalion dropped at bottom and top village will then converge to finish off the rest of the terrorist.

Sunil finally cautioned them that the most important part of the plan was to ensure safety of the captives at the top before the terrorist get any whiff of what's happening. Otherwise they will immediately kill the captives which will defeat the chief objective of the mission.

Everyone nodded their consent to this.

Sunil Singh then took out a small bag in which sat a power phone transmitter. He switched it on, and it got connected immediately."

Sunil Singh said "This is Red Fox," Over.

A static voice came over the "Go ahead," Base here.

Sunil Singh taking out an instrument, detailed their coordinates in a scientific manner. He then instructed the person at the other end to keep a battalion of commandos ready. On signal from him, one half should be dropped at the given locations. He continued that the third helicopter should then bomb the terrorist hideout which will fall between the smoke screen. When it was clear that the base had understood, Sunil terminated the line.

The Chief went out for some time and came back to tell them that he has made arrangements to have the smoke screens to go up at the prescribed locations as and when they signal.

Though tense, everyone felt they had a highly workable plan in hand and felt that it had to be only executed with precision.

To diffuse the tension the Chief arranged a tribal dance for them. Sunil was amused and realised there was something more between Arjun and Rita's relationship, when he saw them dancing very closely amidst the hilarious tribal dancers.

CHAPTER

46

Vijaykar was supervising the hiding places being created in the thick bushes around the pathway under the huge boulders.

He scouted around to check suitable places from where Rani and he could shoot from. The idea was to aim at those people whom the tribals could not kill and who would be of danger to the tribals. Once he found two good places, he got the tribals given to help him to place boulders in such manner that they could shoot from inside with just gaps for seeing and pointing their rifles at the pathway. This way, they would stay protected from return firing of the terrorist.

Vijakar, on hearing some tom tom created by some kind of drums, walked to over to the Chief who was standing with Billoo and asked, "I am hearing some drum sounds now and then. What are they?"

Billoo said, "It is a code amongst us. About two kilometres down the hill a group of our men keep monitoring movement of the terrorist and report to us through this drum coding."

Vijaykar said, 'That's good". He continued, "Please tell them to alert us, be it day or night the moment they spot the terrorists coming towards us. Let them also inform you about the number of terrorists who are coming."

It was about 10.00 a.m. The drums started again. "The chief said, a group of terrorists are coming towards us and they seem to be in a hurry."

How many? Asked Vijaykar.

25, "replied the Chief."

The pathway under the boulders leading from the bridge stretched to about 20 feet. The bridge could only accommodate three persons walking besides each other. He estimated the distance between one following the other to be about three feet. This meant that when the first row reached near the end of the boulder's pathway, the total number of terrorists within the ambit of the snake rain would be 18. It worried him that 7 of them would still be unhurt and could start opening fire at them. Assuming that Rani and himself take four of them 3 would still remain alive and could duck behind the boulders. If that happened, it would be only a matter of time before they over came the situation with their AK 47's. However, he realized that he cannot let the Chief know about it since they might then decide to sacrifice them and simply surrender themselves.

So, he put up a brave face and said, "Fantastic. I was only worried about more than 30 of them coming in at the same time.

The Chief happy with Vijaykar's confidence, patted Vijaykar and led him to top of the boulders where snakes in 100's could be dropped all over the pathway. He showed him their preparations. Places where the tribals will be lying down, the snake pits where the snakes would be kept on both sides of the boulders overlooking the pathway. At a signal from Vijaykar, the tribals would from both sides rain the snakes on the terrorist from the top of the boulders.

Vijaykar enquired the time by which those people will start crossing the bridge.

Billow spoke to the Chief and replied, "They should reach the bridge in about two and half hours.

He then enquired if all the arrows had been given the poison treatment. Billoo replied, "Yes. Everything is arranged as per plan".

To ensure that they did not get caught should the terrorists come earlier, Vijaykar said, "Let your people take positions by 9.00 a.m.

He then went to Rani and described about the positions they had to take. Surprisingly she was in full spirits and ready for the fight.

They checked their rifles and went to their spots with the bullets recovered earlier. Both planned their approach and went back to the hut to take some rest and be prepared for what was to come.

AT 9.00 a.m. both Rani and Vijaykar made their way back to their respective positions. Vijaykar checked one last time and everything seemed to be in place. The tribal men with the Bow and Arrows were well hidden in the bushes. The snakes were full and the men there had taken their positions.

Rani and Vijaykar took up their positions.

At about 9.30 a.m. Vijaykar could see the terrorists coming from the opposite direction. All of them seemed to be equipped with the AK47's. A signal which all of knew came in the form of a bird screeching. Everyone waited now for the terrorists to enter the path way.

The terrorists talking amongst each other, casually entered the path and as planned. When 18 of them were in the pathway, a shower of snakes fell on them. There was chaos and the terrorist on whom the snakes fell were fighting to tear away the snakes away and running helter smelter. The tribals were good in releasing the arrows and all the 18 fell down.

Unfortunately, as Vijaykar suspected might happen, the seven of them at the back sensing something wrong, ducked behind the boulders and were encircling it ready with their AK47. Vijaykar saw one of them coming behind the boulder and firing at the bodies lying on top of the boulder. He took careful aim and released the trigger. The bullet smashed through the terrorist's head and he went down instantly. No one moved for some time. The single shot had unnerved the terrorists.

Then one of them suddenly came into the open and opened the AK47 at the boulder where Vijaykar had shot from.

Rani took careful aim and shot at the terrorist in the open. Since the terrorist was moving in a zig zag manner, Rani's bullet missed his head and instead penetrated the right shoulder. While this was happening, two other terrorists from strategic points opened fire at both Vijaykar and Rani's boulder. The barrage of bullets on Rani's boulder split it and one part of it fell on Rani's head. She fell flat. The bullet which found its way into Vijaykar's lodged itself into his right shoulder and he gasped in pain and was unable to move his hand.

Vijaykars worst fear had come true. He realized that Rani was also hurt since she was not shooting any longer. They were now sitting ducks. For the first time, Vijaykar started wondering whether the tribals hiding the bushes could do anything or the bullets ricocheting from the boulders had killed them?

Vijaykar thanked God for what happened next.

CHAPTER

47

Arjun and party left for the tunnel at 5.00 a.m. and reached the tunnel. They were amazed at the excellent job done by the builders in both building and concealing the tunnel. They started their ascent up the tunnel. Bota led the way and others followed. It was dark and all the troop members except for Bota were using their heavy-duty torch. Bota made up his way as if he knew the path by heart.

After three hours of travelling in the tunnel they reached a dungeon in the Castle. Bota indicated them to wait and went out to check if any one was there. Seeing no one, he gave the green signal and all of them came out. Bota took them to the top of the Castle where the whole village could be seen.

Reaching the top, Arjun could see a bridge far away and remembered that Bota had told him that the only other route to the top village was through that bridge.

But something seemed wrong. He took out his binoculars and was surprised at what came into view. On the boulders of the bridge adjoining the pathway to the village from the bridge, he could see lot of tribals lying and waiting for something with snakes wriggling in their hands. They all seemed to be waiting for a chance to release the snakes.

A reflection from some steel from the other side of the bridge caught his eyes. He could see about 30 men making their way towards the bridge with AK47 slung on their shoulder. In an instant he realized that, the tribals were trying to fight the terrorist with whatever resources they could gather. Little did they know that they were no match to fight with the armed terrorists?

A massacre was on hands unless something intervened.

He told Bota about this and all ran down the castle. When Vijaykar shot his rifle for the first time, Arjun's party had almost reached the boulders. Then, Arjun realized that the tribals had two shooters who were well sheltered in specially erected boulders. Arjun told Bota and Hota to go to the tribal Chief and detail him as to who they were. Both sprinted off in the direction of the village.

Then another terrorist suddenly came out and without fear fired at their boulders. Arjun took out his special rifle, took careful aim and fired. The shot caught the terrorist squarely in the chest and he went down like a rock. The whole place remained silent again.

Arjun and Rita were experts in this kind of fighting. So, Arjun told the commandos to protect the two shooters of the tribal team from their back, while both he and Rita fanned out and moved towards the boulders in which the terrorists were hiding. It took another half and hour for Arjun and Rita to kill all the terrorist using their martial art skills.

Both then went to the boulders. Rita helped Vijaykar come out of his hiding place and administered a pain killer which she had in her pocket. Vijaykar once relieved from the pain, inquired about Rani and both made their way to Rani's boulder where Arjun and other tribals were already at work.

Arjun on reaching the boulder realized that the falling boulder had hit her head badly but her pulse looked to be strong. Rita administered her some medicine which seemed to relax Rani who went into a deep slumber.

By the time, the Chief and his people had all gathered around them. Bota introduced Arjun, Rita and his party to the Chief.

Arjun was happy to know from Vijaykar, that all captives were safe. He told the commandos to give Rani and Vijaykar first aid treatment and then took out his walkie talkie and established contact with Sunil. Sunil was very happy that all the captives were safe. He told Arjun to take some rest wait for the air force to drop the battalion of commandos at the top village in accordance with their plan.

CHAPTER

48

Sunil connected with the air force base and told them to execute their plan of action. The air force base advised Sunil to get the smoke screens started in half an hour's time, since it would take the helicopter about 45 minutes to drop the battalions and then bomb the terrorist hideout.

To the precision after 30 minutes, Sunil asked the Chief to signal his people to start the smoke screens.

Sunil Singh was waiting for the helicopters to make their appearance and the attack to start.

Sunil Singh's mobile buzzed. He connected it and it was Taake Singh.

Pressing the green button Sunil Singh said, "Go ahead, this is Sunil listening."

"Sir, I flew last night to Chennai. Due to some kind of food poisoning I was about to pass out. So, I called the local command post and they admitted me in the military hospital and gave me Saline. Now I am fine and wanted to know what to do? asked Taake Singh over the phone."

An alarmed Sunil realized that Taake Singh's life was in danger. He called his Organization's agent in Chennai and gave him the picture. The agent responded, "Go ahead Sir, ask him to speak to me and I will take care".

Sunil Singh waited for Taake call and said, "Call up this mobile number and speak to Mr. Peter Fernando. I have already spoken to him and he will advise you what to do.

Taake Singh dialled the number and got connected to Peter Fernando.

When Taake Singh identified himself, the voice at the other end seemed very alert.

Peter Fenando said, "Take a taxi to Elliot's beach and given that it's raining, no one would be around. You will find an ancient Arch there. Wait in the Arch and we will take care.

Taake Singh reached the arch and waited. The sky was over cast and the lightning and thunder seemed to indicate a heavy down pour. It was already getting dark. Getting restless after half an hour he decided to light a cigarette. Little did he know that the lighting the cigarette saved his life.

Hussain couldn't believe his luck. Kasab's movement had come to a stand still from last afternoon and he and his gang had taken the flight to Chennai and were driving a rental car towards the area where the star was blinking in his device. As he was urging the driver to drive faster, the star started moving. Using the GPS, he started directing the drive towards the moving star. He thanked Allah when the star came to a rest and it took them another ten minutes to reach the Elliot's beach where the star started blinking faster.

He took out a binocular and searched the beach which seemed totally isolated. The Arch caught his attention and he took time to focus on it and found a man sitting there. He took out his night rifle and levelled it at when Taake Singh lit his cigarette. The shocked Hussain realizing it was not Kasab checked his instrument which still pointed to the direction of the arch. He realized if it was not

Kasab, it was essential to take him alive and learn what had happened. He told his driver to direct the car towards the Arch with and told his group that the person should be taken alive and under no circumstances killed. He also cautioned them to be ready for an ambush as an instinct.

An alert Taake Singh stood up and was watching the car come. The car almost came to a halt when Hussain again opened the device to confirm the mark which was green and steady. The led lights from the device bounced off Husain's face. A shocked Taake realized that it was the same face in the photo shown by Paul to him in the hotel and realized his life was in danger. He dashed to the other side of the Arch and jumped to the sand.

Seeing Taake Singh moving, Hussain and his gang got out of the car and were about to run around the Arch in pursuit of Taake Singh. As Hussain got out, he slipped in a slush of mud and fell. This saved his life.

Peter had been waiting for this moment. The snipers were well camouflaged in the sand that even Taake Singh had not be able to make them out in the rain and enveloping darkness. He gave orders and the strobe light came on and focused on the car just as Hussain fell.

The three commandos were instantly shot dead all of them while Hussain in his fallen position shot the strobe light and it was total darkness. He realized his weak position and took to the sea in huge strides.

Before the snipers could get the light working again, he had taken to the sea and was swimming with rapid strokes and went deeper and deeper into the sea. Once he felt he was out of reach in the darkness, he took out another device from his pocket and switched it on. The signal it started emitting alerted the crew of a submarine camped deep in the Bay of Bengal and it started moving towards its target.

The police gathered the dead bodies and the Police commissioner took Taake Singh to his office where he confirmed that the person Hussain, he had seen in the car was not one amongst the dead.

Taake Singh wondered where Sunil Singh and Arjun were at that moment.

CHAPTER

49

Exactly after the 40th minute of Sunil's talk with the air base, while one helicopter was dropping a battalion of commandos at the top village another one was dropping a battalion at the bottom village.

The third helicopter directed by the smoke screens, was bombing the terrorist hideouts.

Arjun commanded the battalion to descend wiping out any terrorist who might come their way. He told them to be a little careful when they came near the smoke screens since their colleagues from the bottom of the village might come face to face with them.

The head commandant said, "Don't worry Sir, we have been totally detailed on the plan and with a smart salute led his men over the bridge to begin their descent.

Arjun and party along with Vijaykar, and Raj Kiran took leave of the Chief of the top village and made their way through the tunnel to reach the bottom village. Rani was being carried by two tribal in a stretcher.

Soon as Arjun and party entered the bottom village, Sunil along with the Chief of the bottom village greeted them and told them that the operation was a 100% success.

Sunil further said, after elimination of the terrorist, both the battalions have regrouped and are making their way back to a base from where they would be picked up by the same helicopters.

Half way down Rani seemed came to her conscious and insisted on insisted on walking down.

She was delighted when Vijaykar took her hand and when they were alone, she enveloped him with a deep kiss. A blissful Vijaykar joyfully enjoyed the kiss.

162

CHAPTER

50

New Delhi – PMO's residence.

It was time for celebration. The Prime Minister was hosting a special party to thank all involved. The Prime Minister, Home Minister, The Chief Minister of Maharashtra, their families were a part of the celebration. Sunil, Arjun, Rita and the SSA Chief was also present.

The Prime Minister began: Let's offer prayer to those commandos who lost their life's or got hurt during these particularly trying times.

As the audience finished praying in silence, a deeply contemplative Home Minister with mixed emotions tears flowing in his eyes, got up said Jai Hind to a thunderous appreciation from the audience.

He went on to say, "I promise on my Home Minister's berth that I will put in all efforts to ensure this situation never repeats itself".

The Chief Minister got up told that something always come of the bad times as well. I have also learnt in a personal conversation between the Home Minister's daughter Rani and my son Vijaykar, that, they are in love with each other. However bad eve's dropping is, I couldn't help overhearing it by accident and I was really happy. Rani I have always found to be a lovely well behaved and intelligent daughter. It will be my pride in asking the Home Minister for the hand of his daughter to my son.

The Home Minister couldn't believe the look of happiness which had come into Rani's face ever since the baby was lost. The Home Minister caught in mixed emotions with tears flowing in his eyes embraced the Chief Minister and said, "you have brought life back into our family."

The whole audience stood up and clapped.

Sunil took the stage and invited the surprised Arjun and Rita to the floor for a dance and the audience was presented with a scintillating performance by the love birds. Rita realized their invitation by Sunil didn't seem to be an accident. She stopped and whispered something to Arjun's ear.

While Arjun made his way to Vijaykar, Rita took Rani by her hand and soon Vijaykar and Rani were dancing around in the central stage. They looked to be partners by nature.

Everyone was in a jubilant mood and enjoying themselves thoroughly.

The atmosphere went for a spin when the little Raj Kiran ran around with a snake dancing in his hands. As people screamed and were about to run Sunil announced don't worry, it's not a poisonous snake but a new present to Raj Kiran by his tribal friends.

⬤◆⬤

CHAPTER

51

PoP Headquarters - Abbotabad

Ghani told the muscled hunk accompanying him; remember the promise I gave you when you were 13 years old. The hunk bowed and kissing the old man on both cheeks, asked eagerly, "Has the right time come?"

Ghani smiled and asked him if he had a fool proof plan to take India destabilization to the next height.

The Hunk replied, it was ready, even before I was called in to eliminate Kasab".

Ghani gestured him to wait till green lights up and then come to the room it will lead you to through a tunnel. Hussain had not known about this despite living in the mosque for five years. With his heart beat soaring he waited excitedly.

The PoP was assembled inside. All the members were grim.

Qureshi, addressed them,

"My Dear Members,
Our mission has failed. But don't worry. We have news from our intelligence that Kasab's trial will not be taken up for the next few weeks. The ruling party in India is against it and have decided to keep postponing it till next elections. Above all, our mole's is still in place. I rise to win your vote of confidence to proceed further.

Ghani waited till the Qureshi finished his address. He was seated in his usual place at the top of the conference table. He got up. Silence prevailed as Ghani took out a cobra and pointing it at Querish's head, pulled the trigger. Qureshi's head took the blow and he toppled over.

Ghani broke the shocked silence, "There is no space for failure in this Chair."

'I am afraid we need a new head of certain calibre.'

Pressing a button, he slowly made his way to the entrance. On hearing footsteps from the other side opening the door he turned and said, "Here comes, your new Chief."

The hunk of a man walked in majestically. Ghani gestured the hunk to take the head seat.

To Hussain, it was the seventh heaven. He walked authoritatively to the head chair and said, "Allah Ho Akbar". Everyone present said, "Allah Ho Akbar".

Taking the seat, he said, "let us move on, a new chapter has begun."

"Allah Ho Akbar" said everyone, and Hussain's plan was taken up for discussion.

CHAPTER

52

Mole's Residence

His heart broke when he saw the newspapers' headlines that the Pakistan Ex Army Chief Qureshi had passed away.

The "Well Wisher of Pakistan and India was no more". They had been partners of a strange kind. Both didn't want their country to be hurt at the same time saw nothing in using it to their advantage.

His secure phone rang. He couldn't believe it. It was as if Qureshi was calling.

Cautiously picking up the phone he said, "hello."

The voice was clear and precise. I am the telecommunication expert who helped Querishi in his secret communications. I have also been inducted into PoP of late. It was Qurreshi who got me on board. He has detailed everything about your cooperative methods and has assigned me to take over his position on his death.

He did not die a normal death but was shot dead by Ghani. The King is dead. Long live the King.

The Mole chuckled. God whether it be Krishna or Allah seemed to be on his side. He said let's cherish, and uttered "Long live the

King" and may the day come when the Indians and Pakistani's reunite. Till then I shall live up to "Make hay, while the Sun Shines".